ULTIMATE RECKONING
By
Margaret Afseth

ISBN: 978-1-927828-51-9

Publisher's note: This novel is a work of fiction. Names, characters, places and incidents are either products of the author's imagination or used fictitiously. All characters are fictional, and similarity to people living or dead purely coincidental.

This book is dedicated to my two sons. They often swim against the current of life, viewing situations differently, but I love you each dearly. You are my treasures. Thank you for your constant support.

TABLE OF CONTENTS

PROLOGUE:

When they thought of home, each pictured it differently. That was their first mistake. The second glitch in the method, was the portal performance. A five year old may be powerful, but when the directions are muddled, how could a small girl plan the destination; how could Nitha possibly know where the end should be? Especially, when she had never been there.

The center circle was the three girls; the next, held four boys. Surrounding them, their four parents.

Of the children, seven year old Willow was the only one who had experienced life on planet Earth; so she was their guide. When Momma Gem said, 'think of home,' she first thought of the ocean, where she had been swimming with her father, even from an extremely tender age. The boat they last sailed on, was her most recent recollected residence...

But wary, they might land in water, and not wishing to drown her friends, she rejected that memory, and so, at the last moment, opted for a long forgotten recall of her younger momma, from her baby years...

The result was, that city was where she directed her sister to take them.

However, there were other minds involved; thinking not of home, but what such a habitant might be like...

****

E-ri landed alone, with a jar, on the sand bar of a river bank. He went sliding painfully a good ten yards, to thud against a ramshackle, abandoned tool shack, coming to rest with skinned thighs, and scraped lower back. And, he was no longer wearing his animal hide shorts.

The last thing he wanted was to be buff naked. Not now, at the age of fourteen! He resolved, he would find garments, if he had to steal them!

4

Above, Sea gulls circled, their raucous calls resounding. E-ri looked around for the others.

Not even Willow had come along on HIS ride.

****

Peek felt strange. He was now twelve.

He opened his eyes, his face buried in gray smothering ash. When he raised it, he could still hear the far away rattle of gun fire.

For a second, he wondered, if he had been left behind.

He remembered vaguely, at the very last second, of the journey through the dark, shifting tunnel, letting go the hands nearest him. He had been trying to think of human beings with skin the color of his own. That was where he had wanted to go.

Am I still with E-ri, and Willow? No one else here...

Where are Storm and Lee? Nitha, and...Thea?

I seem to be alone...

Peek coughed hoarsely, attempting to rid his lungs of the dust in the air; gazed about him, puzzled; confused. Trying to see through...smoke?

Where am I?

There were damaged buildings in the distance; rubble and bricks all about him; a path strewn with debris: broken wooden frames; twisted metal bars sticking up out of the ground.

What is this place?

Still the rattle of weaponry; the repercussion of a explosion...

But there were no trees, nor the normal call of an animal; not even the unpleasant growl of a dangerous predator.

As Peek sat hesitant, a rough hand grabbed him from behind, and shook his shoulder. The voice that followed it, was speaking foreign words, yet the boy could understand them, by reading the thoughts behind them.

"Come, boy! You can't remain here, in the middle of a battle zone. You'll be certain to be killed. Did you lose your parents? Come along with me. I know where to go..."

Peek looked back, and up, as the man continued; he was too tired to follow the rest of his ramblings.

He rose to his feet, in the grip of the fist on his arm, following along hesitantly; stumbling at times, but the man would pull him up each time, and carry on. His benefactor wore something like a loose, dingy, grey robe, that covered most of his body; sandals on his feet, and a towel-like head covering tied with a rope. The skin that Peek could see was dark brown; the other hand held a rifle on a thin leather strap.

"We need to get you some clothing...you can't go around stripped to the skin. What's the matter with you? When you fled, why didn't you slip something on?"

If Peek hadn't been taught to read minds, he would never have picked up half the man said. The language was as unlike the speech of Azure Blue, as mind-talk was to a spoken word.

Not to mention, not once, did the man allow him a chance to answer.

Peek tried to glean where he was, from the mind of his companion. All he was able to pick up, was this was a place called...Syria.

And the soldiers, and leaders here, were trying to purge the population of malcontents...although, they appeared to not care if they killed whole families to do it.

****

"Go to a place where there are others like me!" Lee thought desperately, just before Peek let go his hand.

When he found himself in a store front window, naked on a tattered couch, Lee had the presence of mind to steal clothing.

He stepped over a ledge, into the darkened interior beyond, hearing the warning clang of an alarm in the air.

He sensed what it meant; he was an intruder; he didn't belong there. The half Asian boy sped into action.

All he could find were cut off jean shorts, frayed along the bottoms. For some reason, he had grown much bigger, at least twice his original size...as if, he had aged to...twelve?

No way!

He finally found a pair that fit, and quickly, donned them. Then, as he heard the squealing of tires around the corner, Lee, again, stepped through the window, and into the street, fleeing in the opposite direction.

****

Storm tossed around in the stream of ever shifting locations. His view of the world, they were suppose to go to, muddled. He had no inkling of the area where he should end, so he simply tried to concentrate on following through the vortex. When Gem had said, 'think of home', he had little idea of where he might fit in. He had so often heard himself referred to as a Neanderthal, by the invading soldiers, he was of a mind, that he would be unwelcome, where ever he landed. Thus, when he dropped into time again, it was to arrive on the grounds of an amusement park, situated in an open field; a circus of animals and freaks.

****

Thea and Nitha came out together, still holding hands. Their idea of Willow's Earth home was a place where young girls were exploited.

They came down, thudding rather violently against dirty payment, somewhere in the red light district of an unnamed city.

Eleven now, their bodies were just budding; the curves slightly beginning to show. Before they could crawl away into the nearby alley, a slurred, drunken voice broke the silence.

"Hey! Now, what we got here? You two lost, or what?"

A trembling hand caught at Nitha's long black hair, keeping her stationary. Shocked by the cruel action, she gasped aloud, but made no other sound; too terrified to move, never having be so manhandled before.

Thea looked up, horrified, as well. Up the dirty pant legs, past a huge beer belly, to a scruffy, whiskered face on a street bum. She grabbed at her companion, ripped her free, and turned to escape, with the usual method, she used back home.

But...nothing happened.

"I can't jump," she moaned in mind-talk. "My energy is too depleted from travelling through the portal." After a moment, she added: "I can't even compel him...or even read him."

"Oh, help!" Nitha shouted, fearfully, in mind words. Only Thea could hear. "What do we do?"

"Hide!" returned Thea, desperately.

As the girls scrambled away from the man's reach, he ogled them.

"Ooee!" he chuckled, with delight. "How about that? Two bare bums; one in blue; the other pink. Got a little boy-girl color going here. I like that!"

Mortified, as realization struck, Nitha transmitted telepathically: "Oh! Gosh! Thea. We don't have a stitch on!"

"And..." Thea agreed, pulling her friend through an open cardboard box, then behind a metal dumpster. "We are no longer five. I think we are...eleven!"

Holding their collective breath, the girls sat there, trying to look smaller, awaiting the worst.

****

"What's this?" the mob boss demanded, as the wino entered, dragging two naked girls by the hair; one in each hand.

They were scrawny, under developed, and one so pale blue, it appeared, he had found her hiding in a refrigerator unit.

"You expect me to pay you for this? Why the one is so blue, she looks frozen."

"You could use her, as a special one, boss," the bum suggested.

His employer shook his head, looked to the beefy protector at his side, who grinned knowingly, but didn't speak.

"Maybe," the boss man said, considering, then shook his head a second time. "Nah. I might take the dark haired beauty...there's plenty call for one her age..." His eyes bore into Nitha, and she cringed. "What's your name, little dove?"

Nitha shook her head; she knew, the moment she opened her mouth, because she was so afraid, she would certainly stutter.

Thea spoke for her. "She can't speak..."

"What? She dumb?"

"I talk for her, and...to her."

"No! No!" shouted the seated man behind the desk, making the girls tremble in their skin. "Don't need two joined at the hips!" He shook his head again, and seemed to calm. "So...what are your names?"

"I'm Thea. This is Nitha..." Thea gestured to the darker skinned girl at her side.

"Right. Might be a nice touch," pondered the boss. "Helpless, dumb...good for the protective sort. So...we have a broken dove, and a...ghost. I'll take the silent dove...but, not the bossy sassy."

"What am I to do with the cold one?" asked the wino, hesitantly.

"Don't care," returned the boss. "Just get it out of here."

"Do I get something for the pretty one?"

The boss shrugged, thought a moment. "Give him some grub," he ordered of the pug-faced man at his side. "And, take this one." He pointed to Nitha. "And get her something pretty to wear..."

As the girls were pulled apart, Nitha to one door, Thea pushed toward the outside entrance, Thea tossed back over her shoulder, a reassurance to Nitha, in mind-talk.

"Soon as I get free, and get enough energy, I'll find you; come and jump you away from here..."

None of the men were aware, any thought words had been spoken.

"Okay," agreed the other girl, silently.

Yet, fear still remained, in both girls.

Chapter 1

When she entered it, this world felt frigid; inhospitable. Like an infant new born, she plunked out on the cold tile floor, from the warmth of the escape portal worm hole of the other world, into the cooler atmosphere of Earth.

She had been told to think of home, and she had envisioned her momma holding her for the first time as a baby...her very first memory. But, this time, there were no arms about her; no comforting kiss of fondness, only hard, icy floor beneath her naked bottom, as she jarred to rest in this future time, and space. And...

She was no longer an infant, but a teen of thirteen...

What travesty was this? She had last been seven.

Where am I? Why am I older?

This body was much more mature, shapely. She had breasts!

Can't stay like this. Need to cover me...

She had landed beneath a sterile white table. Willow sought to peer out at her surroundings. The room was filled with rows of small, raised bassinets, occupied by the tiniest infants imaginable. There were no adults around.

I must be in a nursery? But, why?

The more urgent question was, how was she to get out? And, unnoticed...

Naked as a jay bird, her first order of business must be something to cover her budding reality. She was a woman now, and she couldn't strut around anymore, in nothing but doe skin coveralls. She needed something like Momma Gem had worn, but it was unlikely, in this room, she'd find anything big enough to cover someone her size.

I don't even know how to put on a bra...

At least, down here on the floor, no one had yet noticed her...

The small infants peopling the space were all fast asleep; no relative or parent was standing, gaping awe struck, through the viewing window.

She was safe!

Willow breathed a sigh of relief. Crawling on all fours, she headed toward the only door she could see, across the room.

A feeble, plaintive wail split the silence...then the whole room exploded with sound, as those small ones, beside the culprit, were awakened, by the call of the hungry one.

Willow just made it behind the door, as it opened, and a nurse stepped in, her arms laden with small bottles of liquid. Fortunate for the girl, the caregiver was soon too busy to take note of anyone, but the squalling infants.

For a moment, Willow was reminded of a flashback memory, she had read from Gem's mind: the two older women, Gem with her white/blue skin, and Willow's momma, known then as Jewel, her skin, like the teen's own, a caramel/cream, both trying to satisfy six hungry mouths, all at the same time: black skinned Peek, and Asian featured Lee; their own daughters, Thea and Nitha; Storm and E-ri. Azure Blue was a frantic place then...only E-ri had been old enough to feed himself.

E-ri...the protector; her self-appointed guardian!

Where is he?

Chapter 2

"Think of home, Willow!" Momma Gem had ordered. And this was what had come about...

But, E-ri found this world freakish! He did not view it as a cozy, comfortable habitant.

As he walked the city streets, among the people, watching them, their behavior was most odd. Many moved along with a tiny colored rectangle pressed to their ear, or had an almost invisible ear piece attached beneath their hair. At first, E-ri thought they were talking to the air, or addressing him, until he found out otherwise. Finally, he realized, they were using a communication device, that allowed them to talk to someone on the other end. It was called a cell phone.

Some held a device in their hands, walking along, playing games on it. They even stepped into traffic, unaware they were in danger, until they were honked at.

If they did not use it in any of these ways, the cell phone was in their pocket, wires leading to ear buds under hats or hair, their eyes staring blankly ahead, as the person listened to their favorite tunes.

Should someone have no cell phone, or be unable to obtain such recorded music, they might desperately resort to carrying a blaring 'boom box', in a backpack on their back. E-ri actually passed such a person. As the loud tones pounded in the air, she walked by, marching to the beat of the resounding blast.

As if all this was not bad enough, the atmosphere around E-ri was filled with odious, obnoxious smells: body sweat, overpowering stale perfume, smoke, and gas fumes from the vehicles constantly passing by. The sound of swishing tires; screeching brakes; insulting, derogatory comments, as irate drivers swore at those in the way, also assaulted his senses.

Through all this, no one noticed him; never perceived the white/blue shade of his skin. They didn't even see him. It was as if, he were walking invisible.

Gem, Jewel, Brad, and even Willow, had painted a completely different picture of Earth. They had thought it an exceedingly scenic, pleasant place to live, but...they had left a lot... understated. This was a noisy, fetid, unsociable, impersonal, ugly place to be. Either much had changed while the humans had been away, or E-ri had not landed in the Americas.

This city was crowded with all nationalities; the others had prepared him for those of mostly Caucasian origin, but here were presently: skins of every shade of brown, and black; the sallow tan of Asian, and the tanned of aboriginals. E-ri actually fit in, his white/blue skin, just another variation. And hair was no problem, either...why, some even wore theirs in purple shades, streaked in pink.

As people rarely looked at you, anyway, everyone dwelling in their own reality, E-ri found it easy to walk among them. He noticed the newly budding tree, the just emerging beautiful flowers; he heard the cheerful chirps of the song birds in the bushes...but others saw none of it.

Such a shame...So different from Azure Blue.

On his home planet the trees trunks were purple; the upside-down branches sporting leaves of copper, mauve, and rust; the sky, turquoise, displaying a tangerine sun, and at night, you had two moons, and stars, aligned in circular rings about the planet.

E-ri sighed with the yearning of home sickness.

Oh, well...the only reason, he was staying in this stifling, dirty city was to find Willow. He could sense her here...

No one here used mind-talk; and they seldom spoke verbal, so he could ask no questions. To E-ri that was isolating, restricting; excluded him. It created a huge vacuum that ached in his chest.

He was pining for his sisters; his foster brothers, but especially...Willow. Tears formed in his eyes.

Where are they?

Momma Gem, and Poppa Loni had taught them all; it was unfair, and rude, to read the thoughts, or memories, of those around you, without their permission, but these people all left their thoughts unguarded; let their thinking go rampant, though most minds...were simply, vacant, much of the time.

Surely, here, Poppa won't punish if I read...to understand where to go; how to find the others...

He had been walking long enough now, to build up his energy, to be able to jump...just once.

E-ri opened his mind, expanded the field...and immediately found where Willow was. Then, shocked by what he saw, he gasped aloud, and abruptly closed away the view.

He had never expected to find her naked, and...as a woman.

But, he should not have been surprised; he had come through unclothed, and older, as well. As he passed by a street market, he had taken overalls from a rack, and was now, wearing the ill fitting bib-trousers, that rubbed and chaffed at his skin.

E-ri closed his eyes. He could still see Willow standing there, in his mind's eye.

Wow! She is sooo...beautiful! Her skin looks smooth, and so...caramel gold.

With a snap, he closed away the vivid image.

He had gotten the location, just by seeing her. E-ri teleported into the room where she was dressing.

Willow did not notice him as he arrived, slowly, soundlessly, materializing behind her. Her back was turned to him. She already had a pair of blue jeans on her shapely hips, and was struggling with something her mind called a bra, but it didn't seem to fit her. It was made for a much larger woman.

Frustrated, she finally gave up, threw away the garment, picking up a sweater, instead. As she pulled it over her head, E-ri went invisible, fading, and blending, into the wall of the small locker room.

He would give her a moment to become calm again, before revealing himself.

E-ri knew, he couldn't jump away with both of them. They would be forced to walk out of here together, and...that might prove difficult to explain, should they meet anyone.

Chapter 3

A luminous light image appeared against the twilight back drop, blue/white skin glowing in the half light. Gem was first; this had been her garden; what she thought of as home.

Loni was only minutes behind her. Though it was already growing dark, he could see the shapes of green trees, flowers of many colors; a waterfall pond visible in the moon glow. This storybook cottage had been owned by Gem with her first husband. Loni knew, Sam had dedicated his short life to building all this for her.

No wonder, she considers this home...

But, it wasn't home to him; didn't look anything like what they had left behind. On Azure Blue the foliage was always rust, mauve, or reddish-orange; the setting sun would be a tangerine globe, with two moons chasing each other, hanging just over the horizon; the night sky sporting rings of stars around his planet.

It was only minutes, and he was longing for the place where he had grown up.

However, this would never be Azure Blue; this was Gem's home planet...Earth. Dark...dangerous; where more evil existed then Loni felt he could tolerate. He had seen what they did here...in her memories.

The soldiers that were chasing them came from here...that spoke volumes.

Yet, this had been the safest place to go...their only escape.

Gem stood there gazing about her dream garden; the pale ice-blue of her skin reflecting in the moon light, her blond/white curls tousled.

Because of genetic manipulation, she had changed to his coloring, his inner, alien, physical blueprint, when his DNA had been introduced into her system.

17

As he arrived, her back was to him; both had somehow lost their clothing; they were as naked as the day they were born.

The pair had come through a worm portal. Thea, their own daughter, and Nitha, with her half-sister, Willow, the daughters of Jewel and Brad, in a triple symbiotic unity, had formed the escape tunnel they fled through at the last minute.

The girls, still mere infants, only five and seven, when they left, had not been strong enough to hold the portal open long, so Gem had been psychically supporting the young females. He had, also, but in a more limited way.

Due to this strain, when the elder pair entered the teleportation opening, they had barely enough energy to jump in, and follow the continually shifting vortex.

Loni watched as Gem swayed, unsteady on her feet. He held his breath, waiting for her next action.

Gem finally folded, as her energy drained away completely. Like a rag doll, she went limp, in a dead faint.

Loni knew it wasn't safe to touch her; she could easily drain what little energy remained in him, but he took the chance, anyway.

He reached out, just in time, to catch her.

Loni deemed, it unwise, unsafe, to remain in this vicinity, at the place they had come out of the portal. The soldiers might be following...this was where Gem had first encountered the Overseers, that had brought her to his world. Here, they had killed Sam, the love of her life, and kidnapped her. Some of them, might still reside in the area; be lurking in the shadows.

Loni scooped Gem's slack body into his arms, but not having the energy to teleport with her, he took off running toward the north end of the town.

Though the Overseers had once tagged Gem, Loni had long since removed the device, but the color of their skin would easily betray them both...they could not go unnoticed. They would be recaptured, tortured...experimented upon. At the very least, they would be caught, and questioned by human police...

They had to get out of this village...

He fled, with every bit of speed he could muster, running with his burden, so fast, his image blurred, seeming as if they were but a steak.

Until...

Just beyond the edge of town, exhausted, Loni slowed, and finally stopped, in a stubble field, by a tree enclosed graveyard. He stumbled, and collapsed.

On the uncomfortable, dry, rough straw, that ran around the field, like a path just meant for him, he fell to his knees. The alien man felt little, only depleted of energy; his mind went to another place, as he fell forward.

The unconscious female he carried, slid from his arms. Their ice-blue skin had gone so pale it blended in with the bleached row of wheat, shimmering in the blanketing moon light.

As they fell, both were now completely oblivious to their surroundings.

****

It was midmorning before Loni was aware again. For some time, the sunlight had bathed his body, while he slept the slumber of the dead. It was easy for him to do so; Loni was a deaf mute; yet also, a telepath. The only sounds he heard were from the minds of those around him.

What had awakened him was, he had grown cold. Clouds above had crept in to hide the sun he so desperately needed. It had begun to rain.

From the distance, he read the mind of a man: first birdsong; then the frustrated screech of an annoyed woman, at the discomfort of the sudden wetness dripping from the clouds.

"Oh! Bother! It's starting to rain," cried the female. The language she spoke was the one Gem used when she conversed aloud. "Oh, Oh! I'm getting soaked. My dress will be ruined!"

"Well, head for the car!" ordered the voice of her male companion. "I'll be there shortly."

"But...is it open?"

There was the sound of a click, as of a lock popping open.

"It is now," declared the male. "Go! Go!"

Loni raised his head, and over the weeds of the nearby ditch, he was just in time to see, a bedraggled woman yank open the door of some kind of covered conveyance. From books he had read, he knew it to be called a car, standing in the roadway, next to this field.

Loni ducked down quickly, less he be seen, covering Gem's still quiet form with his own. Waiting.

With his mind's eye, Loni watched the man running through the rain to join the woman. The indignant creature, yanked his door open, got in, and slammed it shut with an unnecessary vengeance. You would have thought, somehow, the vehicle was responsible for the sudden downpour, or had caused their wet predicament.

Loni felt the motor of the automobile vibrate, finally growl to life; the crunch of the gravel beneath the wheels was the last sound he experienced. He shut away from the mind of the man, as the vehicle moved away, sped up, and passed away down the road.

Beside him, his deaf and blind, partner was waking up. The world was as silent to her as it was to him, but...he, at least could see. She used his mind to look at their surroundings.

Gem sighed, weakly.

"Where are we?" she asked in mind-talk. As silently, he answered her.

"On your home world. We came first to your garden; I thought it unsafe...I know, it no longer belongs to you. So, I brought you out here, beyond the town limits...just in case, some of the Overseers are still here."

"Oh, no. I am sorry." Shivering, she abruptly sat up. "I thought of Sam...I'm so sorry. We are...by the graveyard?" A moan escaped her at this realization.

Loni immediately knew, he should have gone much further beyond. This was not a good memory to return to. He couldn't remember...

Why DID I stop here?

****

The rain had stopped almost as soon as the humans had driven away. Loni let Gem lay there resting, as the sun came out again to dry them.

She was not well; he could feel that. The healer of the families, Gem had been much needed, through the incidents prior to their abrupt departure. She didn't just heal with herbs or medicine; she mended by mind, took on the injury; needed considerable time to heal back to normal. And, she had never had that time to recover; not enough, at least.

The Overseers' experiments here on Earth had damaged her considerably. The introduction of Loni's DNA by blood transfusion had caused not only his condition of deafness to be transferred, but caused considerable sight impairment, due to the insertion of the tag into the sinus area behind her eyes. Yet, like Loni, her mind had developed the telepathic, and psychic powers to compensate...even, and especially, the ability to heal. But as she healed back, often, she paid the dearest price for mending others.

As now, without sight, or sound, she could neither see, nor hear, the vibrant, cheerful song birds around them...or take pleasure in the glorious scenery she so enjoyed, as she had during her stay here in the past. Gem soon grew lethargic, taking little interest in seeing through his eyes what was about her.

21

She could follow his thoughts, but chose not to. That worried Loni. He would not leave her until he knew she would be safe, and not injure herself out of desperate, depressive self-pity.

He could let her drain off some of his energy, to increase her stamina, but...without sufficient psychic energy, Loni would, then, not be able even to teleport far.

How long has it been since we had nourishment?

Loni needed to find something to fill their bellies...

It wasn't like it had been back on Azure Blue. He not only didn't have weapons to hunt; he realized, here, it was a practice either forbidden or controlled, and to use psychic means...he needed to build up his sun energy...

Loni didn't dare leave Gem, not even to jump away to a store.

****

His Gem had always been the center of their universe; the organizer of his amalgamated family. She had worked tirelessly for his welfare, and that of the children, that had been forced, by circumstances, into their care. Ever since the rescue of the small ones, Loni had relied on her. They had been Poppa and Momma to the orphaned infants, and even though E-ri, had then been already two, and was some help, he had been the only one able to feed himself. Six babies, only three adults to tend them, and little food. But, Gem had been the intelligence, the coordinator. She had brought it all together.

And, right now, he was lost without her. This was her world; he needed her guidance. But, she was unable...even to function. Loni must take the lead.

He knew, they could not remain in this field. Loni bent, and gently kissed the brow of his sleeping mate. He remembered, how she had been chosen for him. They were both merely slaves. Her hands had been bound behind her; she was naked, as she was now. They had stood her behind him, bound his hands around hers with a colored cord, and in the ceremony, the Overseers had forced upon them, they were bound in the symbolism of mating.

In his world, if a male could not get his partner to surrender, another could take her from him, should he choose. Loni had been ever so gentle, so persuasive; Gem had given in; their union was sanctioned. But that had not stopped Galar. That male felt, Gem should have been his in the first place.

Loni did not wish to remember those days, when the separated twins had kept Gem a prisoner...

It almost seemed as if they had gone back to that time. The EM pulse Galar had used to shield his slaughter house had rendered Gem not only powerless, but confused, as well. The effect on Loni, when he tried to rescue her, was to make him as useless as she. Only, when Galar went out from the animal shelter had Loni reclaimed his woman, and...it had been a long, horrid journey back to health.

Now, here on this planet, the atmosphere appeared to have much the same affect. After passing through the portal into this world, Gem...and even he, seemed to have little or no abilities as they'd had in the past.

Perhaps, these would return, with absorption of sun rays, but the weaker orb here did not give off the radiation near as fast, and it took longer to absorb. All Loni could do was teleport, as soon as the sun rose above the horizon. Then from a nearby grocery store, he might steal what they required.

He knew that would be considered wrong; he would be viewed a criminal. On his world, the way they had set it up, all food and clothing was free; all anyone need do is help carry the workload. On this world their ice blue skin coloring, and cat-like eyes would brand them. The humans would call them predators, whether so or not.

They had to survive.

This was unfamiliar territory, even for Gem; she had been a normal human being when living here last time.

It was different now.

Gem sighed, awoke, and stretched. He made her eat the hand full of berries he'd gathered from the bushes near at hand.

As she savored them, Loni inquired: "Do you want to visit the grave of your first love?"

He knew that was a custom here.

She shook her head.

"No...I think not. Memories hurt. His spirit was never here...it has been more than twenty years..."

He sat silently by her, waiting.

After they had been quiet for some time, he suddenly asked:

"Do you feel it, too?"

"The presence of extreme evil? she returned. "I thought, at first, I had imagined it, but...yes, I feel it...like an overpowering stench. Now that the Overseers are cut off from their world, they have taken over this one..."

Loni shook his head in regret. "It seems far more prevalent...this resident wickedness. Worse than it ever was in the domes back in my world."

"Perhaps, we simply didn't notice?"

"No, I think not. It is worse here. I cannot even connect to the Maker in this world. It is like, it now belongs to..."

"On my world it is called...the devil...or Satan."

Loni shivered visibly. He rose to his feet, helping her also to stand.

"We need to move from here. It is not safe to stay in the open."

Arm in arm, they set off at a slow pace across the field.

She was so utterly weakened.

****

Soon, they found a road. Following it, night time was quickly upon them. At long last, they found an old abandoned ramshackle barn, where they took shelter from the elements.

He piled hay in a corner for her, so she could rest. Then, he sat nodding, but still somewhat alert, guarding his greatest treasure.

The days passed, and she slept on. Each morning, just when the sun came up, and before any human roused, he would teleport to a nearby empty market, gather what edibles were available. Only a few, mind you, so they would not be missed. Just enough to feed them for the day. He also found clothing for them.

But Loni never went far; and not for long.

Chapter 4

The young black boy, Peek, sat on the examining table, his bare legs swinging. Though they thought he couldn't understand the tongue, the boy could hear the two physicians discussing him from the next room. It was a foreign language they used, but as always, he had quickly picked it up by reading their minds.

"This boy is not normal," declared the one man. "I'd like to hold him back, and do more tests..."

"Did they do the blood tests?" The first acknowledged, they had. "Are the results back?"

"Yes. That's the main reason I'd like to keep him. I thought at first the samples were corrupted, but...someone must have been doing experiments... The little beggar...the blood work, shows signs of Avian DNA."

"What! That's not possible. Part...bird?"

"It's there. I did the tests myself...three times over!" exclaimed the first physician.

"Someone in this country has that kind of science knowledge to do something like that?"

"Shhh.." cautioned the first. "Someone might be listening..."

The other dropped to a whisper, but Peek could still follow the conversation by mind-read.

"Never realized this country had such labs... Is it possible, that is why, this war is being fought? To cover up what they are doing here?"

Silence reigned for seconds. Finally, the second man asked another question:

"Was he with the refugees?"

"We found him more or less alone, off by himself, in a room with the older boys."

"You have examined him?"

"Yes. His bone structure is peculiar, especially his back. The shoulder blades extend down in ridges, at his sides...goes right to the hip, like a pocket. It is soft to the touch, encasing or hiding something..."

"Hiding...what?"

"Well...until I can get him under the knife, I can only speculate..."

"So, how...what?" his companion exploded impatiently.

"Well...he's still quite young...around, maybe, twelve. He's gone through a tremendous growth spurt in the last week. I think...he's developing...wings."

The other laughed outright. "Holy...holy! A monster? Like the...Syrian...legends? What were they...were they trying to create the mythical creature?"

"Have no idea. It could simply be the result of an injury. He was seriously damaged, at some point. His face gives evidence of that."

"How?"

"I think, he was shot. And who ever removed the bullet, did not have the expertise. I'm sure you have noticed one eye is half closed, and that side of his face sags...I think, he had a stroke during the procedure."

"The very fact he was shot, terrifies me. It tells me, he was considered dangerous, or was uncontrollable, and got away...but...now, he's handicapped?"

"Maybe," agreed the other.

"But, is it enough so...he may not develop farther?"

"That too, must be determined. I suggest, we lock him in an abandoned room in one of the damaged buildings...until we can use an operating room...and determine for certain."

"Do so!"

Peek could have saved them the trouble; he could have shed light on the truth, but no one asked him. They simply assumed he was ignorant of his past.

These men were no different than the Overseers from the stories he'd seen in Poppa Loni's mind.

Peek could have told them, he had been born on another world. They would never have believed him. The black boy was just one of many babies grown from mixed DNA; an attempt to enhance worker abilities, but the creators of that program had done little monitoring, and expected slim results. Peek knew, he might have yet undiscovered hidden talents, but...wings?

Poppa Loni...and E-ri have none. Do they?

No! They simply teleport!

****

The room was barren; the floor covered by rubble; the outside window missing, shattered. No furniture. That had been gathered away by scavengers.

Depressed, Peek struggled half heartedly with the ropes that cut deeply, binding his hands behind his back. They had placed him in a corner, on the bare floor boards, wearing only a pair of dirty shorts; his feet bare.

The air was frigid; the night outside dark. The sounds of gun fire all around.

I can't get to anyone...can't even hear their minds. Where are the friends I had back on Azure Blue? This is no way to live...

Where is Poppa Loni? I want to go home...but I can't teleport like E-ri...

I can't call an animal to help me...like Lee...

Or freeze ropes, so they fall away...like Willow...

Tears began to slide down his cheeks. His heart had sunk to hopelessness...bereft, broken. For a small moment, Peek wanted to end his misery...the unbearable hurt.

He rose to his feet, awkwardly, his hands still bound behind his back. He walked to the window; stood looking out into the jet black space.

He thought of what the doctors had said.

If they are right...

Oh, Maker. If this doesn't work, I am coming home to you...

Without another thought, nor second of hesitation, Peek stepped off the window ledge, into the obsidian night. His skin blended with the jet black space, as if he had never been there. Not even a cry of fear rent the air, as he passed from sight.

****

He was falling...falling; the wind whooshing through his tight curly hair; brushing icily across his parched skin.

There was a snap, as of a sail unfurling, and...something held him up, like a protective umbrella, but it wasn't a parasol. It was more as a rack of...feathers? Stretching back behind him, moving, as if they had been there, always a part of him.

Peek was floating; gliding, soaring on upward air currents.

HE WAS INDEED...FLYING!

Chapter 5

Going invisible, E-ri followed Willow into the dimly lit truck-stop restaurant. They were blocked by a line of customers, mostly of dark hair, eyes and skin. Not as dark as Peek's black complexion, but of a variety that made them blend with the shadows, until you almost bumped into them. What made matters worse, they wore grey or black, as if they wished to hide from sight.

Not a one was female, and as E-ri gazed about, he noticed a few small children sprinkled among them, hidden behind the legs of its parent, but these too, were all male.

Do humans not feed the females? Or maybe...the dark races don't feed them in public?

It had taken E-ri only a short time to understand two things...three, if you used logic. First, he easily got the verbal and readable language from Willow's mind; second, as a couple, they had no currency, and no means to get it...therefore, thirdly, they were reduced to begging...or trickery, to feed and clothes themselves, which of course amounted to...thievery.

Most important of all, Willow had made it apparent in no uncertain terms:

"We have to disguise you. Your skin, we can cover up, but your eyes stand out like a deer in the headlights." His pupils went vertical, like the slit eyes of a feline.

Rather than wear dark glasses all the time, E-ri's solution to that was, when in close proximity to others, he remained invisible. He was glad this time he had done that, as their surroundings were so darkened, his skin would have glowed; not to mention, his vision might suffer, as well.

A Caucasian blond moved up to the counter, a packet of menu boards in her hands. She surveyed the line of many patrons; her eye lit on Willow standing alone.

"Just one?" she asked. Willow gave a slight nod. "Follow me, please."

E-ri was aware, there were frowns, and grumbles behind them, as they by-passed the others; but he saw the woman had done that because most were groups of many. She had not meant it as a slight.

The attendant led them to a corner booth, near the back entry door, right next to the bathrooms. E-ri was immediately aware of the advantage this gave them.

The booth was obviously meant to seat at least four, and as Willow slid in on one side, and E-ri from the other, the woman added a proposition, as she placed the menu on the table for Willow's perusal.

"There are so many refugees crowding into the place today, we don't have room for their big families... If it was needed, ah...would you be willing to share your table?"

E-ri read what was implied here; from thoughts and knowledge around him. Willow was unaware, what was behind the question.

The waitress expected, like so many other dinners had before her, Willow would generously offer to cover the cost of the entire bill, should the foreigners not wish to pay.

Because of attitudes in their receiving country, the immigrants accepted in, viewed themselves privileged, even expected to be indulged. They assumed meals would be supplied free by any establishment.

It was true, this restaurant's owner had made it policy to prefer the refugees. If the customer could not, or would not come up with the asking prices, or someone else didn't offer to cover it, the cost was to come from the salaries of the servers; their generosity assumed, expected, even forced, upon the workers.

The waitress simply wished to ensure, she would not be the one docked for the extra meals.

Unfortunately, it seemed of little consideration: that all refugees received a large living allowance to cover expenses until they were employed, going on for the first five years or more in this country. Also, most immigrants had considerable holdings in bank accounts back in the country from which they fled; they simply could not yet access it.

Yet here, in this town, they were taking advantage of the local generosity, expecting charity without the consequence of paying it back. They figured it was owed them, after all they had gone through.

And, what all sides failed to realize was, the income for the free handouts from the government, received by the fugitives, was gathered by lowering the benefits, and allowances, of the poor, handicapped, and senior residents born here.

As everywhere, in affluent society, the rich were preferred above the poor. The immigrants with money, the education to fill the best job positions, and the largest families, were the first to be accepted; these were the ones preferred across the nations; the ones now, preying on the generous.

The situation made E-ri livid with anger. He wished he could influence the situation; even stop it. But...he too was a migrant; a predator, preying upon others.

And, he had no support...

Annoyed by the unbalances he had discovered, E-ri silently enlightened Willow.

His companion chuckled at the irony.

She immediately realized; they were about to mirror the behavior of the new refugees.

The waitress was still waiting for her answer, but Willow had no intention of enabling the freeloaders.

Still, she shrugged, and quietly said aloud: "Sure." Pretending ignorance, she added: "Why not?"

E-ri frowned.

How will WE pay?

Wait...and watch...

Only problem...in the end, someone would have to pay. Willow hoped circumstances would be on her side, and bring about fairness.

Would the rich immigrants end up paying for their meals?

Right now, turn about seemed fair play.

E-ri shrugged. Willow knew her world better than he.

A second waitress came to take Willow's order. She asked for a chicken BLT salad, and two milk shakes, one cherry; the other strawberry. As an after-thought, Willow added two huge burgers with fries.

"Hungry, aren't you, honey?" The woman grinned.

Willow innocently smiled back; tongue-in-cheek; literally.

Moments later, the first woman returned, leading three dark skinned scowling males. Obviously, they had been waiting in line, and there wasn't room for them with their other family members. Seating them beside Willow, and handing them menus, the waitress took off again.

A third attendant came to take the orders of these men. The process took considerable time, and effort, as each request was given in hesitant English, interspersed with rapid fire questions to each other in the foreign tongue of the refugees.

No sooner had that server left, then Willow's food arrived.

First; her salad. Willow opened it, and began to eat; ravenously.

The men eyed her with obvious distain; enviously.

From the mind of one male, E-ri read: 'How dare they serve the female first!'

E-ri almost laughed out loud.

Next came the burgers with fries. Willow let them sit there. Both the invisible, and visible, slavered at the aroma of the juicy meat.

The other men eyed the food, but politely waited, though the anger, and indignation was evident on their faces.

E-ri was starving. His tummy growled objection, but he couldn't reach out and take, what he knew was meant for him...

And Willow couldn't reach out and pass it to him, without them seeing.

It would have been easy to sneak a fry, unnoticed, but E-ri didn't want to jeopardize the situation. So he waited, desperately craving the succulent burger.

After a wait of many minutes, he almost went visible.

Boy, wouldn't that freak out these arrogant males.

When the girl brought the shakes, Willow found the chance to pass the two burgers to E-ri under the table. The men had their eyes on the waitress.

"Where is OUR food?" questioned one of the men, frowning broodingly.

The woman laughed. "It will be here directly...Oh, here it is now!"

And in the mix up of the two waitresses, one sliding past the other; the plates being put before the hungry men, Willow passed the fries, and remaining salad under the table to E-ri. He quickly stuffed them into the generous pockets of his coveralls, while Willow caught up one shake; he the other, and both slid under the table, and out the other end.

The two fled along the hallway toward the bathrooms, unnoticed. Then out the back door, and along the back side of the building. Neither breathed a sigh of relief until they were out near the highway again.

Finally, E-ri went visible. Only then, did he jump them to a safer hiding place, in a nearby park. On a bench there, E-ri finally got to eat.

As they did, Willow wondered:

Who finally had to pay?

E-ri answered.

The men. The meals were all added together with the family order...it came from their living allowance.

Willow chuckled.

That definitely seemed fair after all, except...to the poor the allowance had been taken from in the first place. But...one step at a time.

****

Each night Loni probed the darkness for the thoughts of the children. He felt E-ri the most, and longed for his help. The boy had the most powerful mind...and with each search; each repetitious hope, Loni's presence became more evident; E-ri finally got the message.

The boy at last, knew exactly where his foster parents were.

Now, it was just a matter of getting there with Willow. It was too far away to teleport two full grown teens.

Chapter 6

It took Peek many nights after he flew away, to saw his hands free of the bonds. He used a sharp end of a piece of tin from the wreckage of a building. At long last, the rope frayed, and dropped away.

Peek hadn't dared to ask for anyone's help.

When he first landed in the darkness, the black boy knew he had better stay hidden. They would be searching for him.

Each day, he hid among the ruined buildings, watching, waiting for each night. When others slept, he worked away at his bindings, until his hands were free.

During that time, he never spread his wings, nor once flew.

When at last, he was free, he stood to his feet. Walking away into the darkness, his belly grumbling for food. But...he dare not ask for a handout. Peek didn't relish being a prisoner again.

Days passed; at long last, Peek came upon a camp of migrants on the shores of a murky sea. To him, the presence of an inland sea meant there must be other continents; this wasn't the only land. Maybe the others had landed in a more civilized country.

They certainly are not among this strange speaking race...only other answer...they are not on this planet at all.

Peek shivered, trembling at that very thought. Surely, he wasn't the only one that landed here?

A group of families were gathered around a camp fire; soup boiled, giving out a pungent unpleasant odor. Peek crept closer, and was handed a wooden bowl. By this time, the boy no longer felt his hunger. He wouldn't refuse any kind of nourishment.

Peek sat down among the many emaciated children; being small, and as starved as they, he easily blended in.

The bowls were filled with a greenish liquid. When Peek brought it to his lips, he nearly gagged. He moved it back an inch, found leaves and grass floating in the broth.

"Hold your breath," suggested the boy next to him, candidly. "It helps not to smell it." After a pause, he added: "You don't want yours. I'll have it..."

Peek held his breath; raised the bowl once more, and swallowed all the contents in one gasp.

After, he moved to the edge of the crowd, his belly roiling. It didn't take long, and his pilfered meal hit the sand.

The other boy had followed him. From at his back, he spoke:

"First time? You'll get used to it...grass and leaves is all there is left to eat."

Peek trembled; fought back tears...then slunk away into the night to be alone.

Later that night, he crept into the group again, lay down among the older boys to sleep. He made certain his wings were folded away unseen, so no one would know he could fly.

He was aware, he couldn't fly far. He knew his best bet was to be with a group, after all, but he resolved, at the first sign of a surgeon, a doctor, or a white skinned man, he was out of there.

His only thought, now, was to get across the water, to a bigger settlement.

****

It was the middle of the night, of the third day. The noisy, excited chatter of grownups woke Peek. A large boat, with some sort of motor attached to the rear, had come silently ashore. They were taking on passengers.

Peek clambered aboard without being accosted; sat down near a side edge, so if his being there was objected to, he could easily slip into the water, and disappear.

The black boy had never ridden the sea before, and this boat was too crowded; bodies from one side to the other; packed like fish in a barrel. No room at all to breathe.

The vessel rocked from side to side, on huge angry waves; up, down; up, down; up again...then, down.

Like so many others, Peek soon was gagging over the edge. At least, he was at the rim...each time another passenger spilled his meal, Peek found there was renewed reason to follow suit. His misery continued all through the night, appearing to have no end in sight.

While the sky began glowing with new crimson dawn, the overloaded vessel began to sink. Peek entertained the thought to fly away to safety, but there was no room to spread his wings. Just as he was beyond desperate, a large ferry boat topped the horizon.

Within minutes, their burdened miniature motor boat was surrounded by all manner of rescue crafts, some small, others large, some even huge.

The passengers were anxious, desperate to get to safety; few would wait, so they crawled over each other, clawing for purchase; caring little for the welfare of others. Children, small babies, young girls, were thrown to the men in the other boats, to catch.

Peek tried to be patient, stay calm, but his heart was pounding so fast, so loud, he was barely aware of the noise around him: shouts, and frightened screams, bawling infants; angry men and fearful mothers.

At long last, a man reached a hand to Peek. The hand slipped...and the black boy went into ice cold water. His heart went to panicked beat, as the murky water surged over his head. Reaching up above, over his head with both hands, in terror, Peek searched for rescue...a hand grabbed the tousled fuzz on his head.

He came up gasping, bodies floating around him; some dead; some living. He was one of the lucky souls.

A blanket draping his shoulders, shivering uncontrollably, Peek finally found himself on a big ocean liner heading to a new shore.

He was warmer by the time they landed; walking toward a huge warehouse type building, when he spied those he most feared...doctors in white coats.

The crowd was thick about him; an alleyway loomed to his right. He turned to face that way, his heart doing a drum roll. His feet moved in time to it, and still clutching the blanket he'd been given, Peek ran with all his might.

He disappeared within the shadows before anyone noticed.

****

Once more, Peek went into hiding. By day, he lay low; at night, he flew...until he had no energy left. Each morning, he found a new haven: a ditch, a cave, an old abandoned building. He ravished the garbage piles and bins for scraps of tossed away food; fed himself that way, limitedly.

When he finally came to the edge of a city, he found a field containing dozens of huge boats with stationary wings, that took on passengers, and flew off into the sky. He knew, he still must stay hidden, so he slipped aboard, among the cargo, in the belly of one of the awkward looking machines.

He felt when it lifted into the sky. The ride was rough, but much easier than the boat ride. He wasn't near so frightened this time; Peek knew, if it threw him out, he could at least fly away.

It was dark when they landed. Peek stayed hidden until everyone had left, then sneaked out to fly away; soon he was just a black bat-bird receding into the distant obsidian night.

****

It was well into a month or more, before Peek learned he had come at last to the Americas.

By then, he also knew, if any of the others had landed on Willow's planet, this would be the place he would most likely find them.

Chapter 7

Trumack had been born into a military family; the third of five boys. His father, grandfather, and great grandfather before him, had all been military commanders, and even further back, there had been a slave trader pirate; two generations ago, a great uncle was a member of the Ku-Klux-Klan.

Oh, yes; he came from a long line of those who weeded out the undesirables, therefore, it was only logical; he was excellent material for the Special Forces.

His ancestry was first German, but he had been born in the U.S. of A; in the state of Texas, to be exact. His birth mother was pure Austrian, but his father had considered her beneath his station; only existing to father his male line. From an early age, Trumack realized, he must prove himself. His father's prejudices swiftly became his own: women were there to serve him; blacks were mere stupid slaves; and chinks were always dumb kitchen staff, in his eyes.

That was until, he went into the U.S. army, where the rule was: all men were mistreated equally.

When the Special Forces took him in hand, old attitudes quickly surfaced; no one considered beneath him was ever accepted to his squad. He soon became the leader of the most deadly group of men in existence.

But even his lineage, family intolerances, and extraordinary training, had not prepared him for his last mission...

That up-side-down world had taken the starch out of his uniform.

When he followed the alien adults, he expected they were heading back to Earth. As Trumack came out of the time tunnel, he landed in the middle of a war zone. He was in a desert; back in his home world again, but...none of his men had followed him through to this side.

Nothing seemed to have changed here. He was now in his element; it didn't even phase him. His tattered clothes, and wounds, he could easily explain away...he had been captured; had gotten away from the enemy. That last fact was the truth...but, who the enemy had been was no one's business, and not to be disclosed under any circumstances.

First; he needed to contact his Superior...

Trouble is: Just what war is this, anyway?

****

"I tell you, sir," Trumack insisted, for the third time. "I'm all that's left of an elite Special Forces Unit; we were on an assignment. I need to report to my Commander back in the States. If you'll just call him; I'm sure, he'll acknowledge me."

He stood before the field officer. In his shredded garments, and bloody face, arms, and legs, Trumack knew, he did not present a believable picture. How could he be taken seriously?

Though dubious, the officer finally placed the call. When he was connected, the man's attitude changed completely.

The conversation was brief; respectful on this end; curt and commanding from the other, as the officer described the man standing before him.

"You do realize," he whispered, as he passed the instrument to Trumack. "You've been missing over six years..."

Brought up short; shocked to the core, Trumack almost blurted out where he'd been.

Six years. Holy Crap! I've been gone that long?

But his training quickly took over.

The field Marshall, with his staff, courteously vacated the tent. Trumack finally turned his attention to the voice of his Superior, on the other end of the line.

"Sir!" Trumack went to rigid attention, as if he were standing before the actual physical person.

****

It was while Trumack was waiting in a bar, for the cargo plane that was to be his ride back to the states, that he met the Italian doctor. The man appeared anxious, nervous around soldiers. Trumack smelled a secret, and that was enough for him to go into investigative mode. After a few drinks, the man was easy to pump.

He and a friend had found an unusual kid: a black boy of about eleven or twelve; deformed of face, with a peculiar abnormality on his back. Trumack knew instantly, this must be one of the alien brats.

Didn't number One nearly kill one of them, back in that other world? Maybe it was only injured...if it survived...

Trumack was intrigued; he arranged to stay another few days, just so he could look into it. It was a good thing he did.

****

They said, they had the boy confined in an abandoned building, but during the night, somehow, he had gotten free.

Trumack asked around among the refugees, and those attending them. The boy had been seen on the shore of the sea, then again among a boatload of migrants on the water. At the port, on the other side, when they had made it to shore, all evidence of him vanished.

It frustrated Trumack. Just like the kids of the alien jungle, this boy had disappeared without a trace.

Where could a kid like that go? He is unfamiliar with the customs of Earth...how did he even get free, in the first place?

Someone is helping him! That whole bloody crew must be in our world.

Trumack finally got his last clue; the boy had been seen in an airport miles away.

Yeah, that figures. Helped, alright!

Trumack suspected the teen had been stowed away aboard a flight to the Americas. He determined to hunt down these unwanted vermin, if it was the last thing he ever did.

But his Superior got in the way...

Trumack was ordered to take some much deserved R and R.

Well, that's okay, too. I'll just do it on my own time...after, I first see my woman...

****

To raze his ire further, Trumack had to hunt down his girl friend, before he could get any sort of action. She was in the process of moving...to Canada, no less; of all the crappy places she could choose from...

He finally found her in a basement apartment in Regina, among unpacked boxes, with a half grown German Sheppard puppy tagging along at her back.

She had gotten a job as a real estate salesperson, and was to start the next day, but Trumack had other plans for her first. He wasn't adverse to her new employment; that wasn't the problem. Just, she could start later...when he was finished with her.

Trumack even brought her pizza...

He made her leave the box of food she was unpacking, on the counter; the open pizza on the table. Right now, he wasn't interested in that kind of stimulant. First, he would relieve the starving inner savage between his thighs; later...there was always time to eat.

She was a good match for him; as hungry and violent, from the long forced abstinence, as he. He came up from two hours of rough pleasure; to a hair raising growl, of pure savagery.

It brought to his mind thoughts of the wolves that had attacked him, back on the other planet. The evidence of their vicious bites still covered his naked body.

That didn't come from my woman!

Trumack shivered at his memory cinema, cringing involuntarily.

He lifted his head and shoulders; gazing about, searching. His eyes quickly lit on the cause.

Across the open space, on the counter in the kitchen, a big mangy cat-stray had discovered a package of raw hamburger, and was yowling as it feasted.

"Where the hell did that thing come from?"

Trumack rose up in one fluid motion, reached for his German luger on the chair, tripped over the mongrel pup, and went sprawling. The cat fled, vanishing soundlessly, somewhere out the open window, never to be seen again.

He looked down at his feet; the dog had pulled the pizza from the table; was in his glory, wolfing down their lunch.

That was the last straw!

Trumack rolled to his side, reached out to the chair, caught up his heavy weapon, and placed it on the forehead of the errant offender. He never heard his woman shouting a warning:

"No! Don't!"

He simply gave way to the soldier's reaction.

The dog had only time to give one frightened yelp. The report was sharp, quick, and loud. The mutt flopped over, a hole through his brain...dead, blood, and brain matter, spattered everywhere.

Then...all pandemonium broke out around them.

This was Canada; Trumack was a U.S. citizen. Guns were carried without thought in his country, but here, there were laws, and rules, against carrying firearms; not to mention openly using them.

It was a good thing the girl friend's apartment was on the ground floor.

Trumack immediately knew he was in trouble, so he did the only thing left to him...he ran.

He caught up his clothes from the floor, and went to the open window. As sirens filled the air, naked as a jaybird, Trumack fled to his car. He pulled away thinking:

Just need to get away, lay low 'till things cool down.

His woman would explain: she had never been in danger. Her man didn't know better; he was from the U.S...the dog had tripped him.

Trumack knew when it all blew over, he could safely sneak back in.

To him, this was all just a lark...

Stupid Canadians!

Chapter 8

Her golden-caramel complexion, brown eyes, and long, straight dark hair drew the attention of all men around her. The fact that Willow appeared alone, walking at the side of the highway, holding a thumb up for a ride, brought most truck drivers to a sudden sliding stop. They usually were thinking: Prostitute.

E-ri saw it in their minds; before the teen ever entered, invisible, into the bed-bench, in the back of the cab. He always remained Willow's unseen guardian...and, got in first.

The semi pulled to a steaming, huffing stop; Willow yanked the passenger door open, and held it wide; waited long enough for E-ri to climb in, finally, stepping up, and inside, herself. She made a show of slamming the heavy door closed again.

The leering look covered the man's moon-like tanned face. He was obviously too intent on Willow's curves, to notice the shift in weight, just before she got in, or see the indentation of the leather back, as E-ri slipped over into the bunk behind.

"Need a little help there, girly?" offered the obese, giant human, his eyes on her rear end, not the closing door.

"Got it," Willow panted, objecting quietly.

"You're such a small little thing...where you heading?"

"Anywhere you are," she replied in a near whisper.

"Ahhh...now, that pleases me."

E-ri knew, if he wasn't along, Willow would be no match for this one; she'd never fight him off.

"Why don't you move on over, now," the trucker suggested. Willow had stayed as close to the far door as possible. "Don't be so shy; I won't bite."

He geared up, and slowly pulled away from the pickup site.

Willow understood fully, just what he was hoping for; she remained as far away from the reach of his arm as she could.

Amazingly, the driver took the hint. From his mind, E-ri read: 'I'll just give her some time.' The cab went silent, and remained so, for many miles. Finally, the big fellow inched his arm across the back seat, reaching for Willow. She paid it no mind, but E-ri wanted to stab the beastie before he could make his move.

"Ah, come on, girly. Don't tease. Come a little closer. I need some sugar as payment..."

Willow remained distant. The man returned his attention to his driving again; his eyes to the road.

Finally, after a long period of no response, the man once more removed his arm. A roadside truck stop restaurant was coming up on their right.

Minutes later, he pulled in to the area.

"How about I buy you dinner?" he persuasively suggested. "You come in with me. I get you anything you want..."

Willow shook her head.

"Okay. I can bring something out...You wait right here in the cab. I'll come back shortly..."

Willow thought for a moment; finally spoke: "Two BIG burgers," she agreed.

Encouraged, the beefy trucker chuckled, and hopped down.

"Okay, sweetie. Fair is fair. Two BIG burgers it is. And...how about fries, and a drink?"

Willow nodded.

"Your first time; isn't it?" The man laughed to himself, slamming the door shut; closing them in.

For long minutes, E-ri didn't say anything, even in mind-talk. They just sat there and waited, but E-ri was fuming.

Why do human men always have their thoughts in their trousers?

"That's where their brains are," Willow replied out loud, giggling at her own joke. E-ri chuckled.

When the trucker returned, he brought the food around to her door, yanking it open, trapping Willow. Her heart took up a rapid staccato beat.

Balancing the tray of food containing at least five large burgers; he handed it up to her.

"How about, while I drive, you feed me, sweetie?"

She took the tray, hesitantly. When he slammed the door shut again, her breath escaped in an explosion of relief.

Willow immediately placed the food on the seat between her and the steering wheel; quickly transferred two hamburgers back to invisible E-ri, before the man got in again.

"Wow!" exclaimed the driver. "Where'd they go so fast?"

"I'll eat them later," Willow declared boldly.

He laughed, and shifted the clutch of the idling rig.

"Put them in your pocket, did you?" He chuckled again. "Okay, darlin'. I drive; you feed me."

But Willow had no intention of feeding this monster. He was intent on getting back on the road, occupied for the moment, so she got away with stalling.

Fifteen minutes passed before the man thought of the food again.

"Time to get out!" In mind-talk, E-ri's voice broke into Willow's thoughts."That is the turn off, just up ahead."

"Okay," she answered quietly, out loud, and the driver thought, she was asking if he wanted to be fed now.

Seconds later, at the junction, E-ri made a silent suggestion to the mind of the truck driver.

"You are very tired...Sleep, human."

As the man slowly nodded off, by mind control, the boy in the back, guided the vehicle; shifting down easily; for he had watched often how it was done; gliding it gradually to a stop, by the side of the road, near the crossroads.

As both teens vacated the cab, E-ri grabbed the rest of the food. As a homecoming offering, his intention was to feed his meat starved parents, when he arrived at his destination.

But he had one more parting gift for their benefactor...

While E-ri moved away down the road, he sent a last wish toward the offender behind him. He imagined in his mind, the man they had left abandoned...castrated.

E-ri could heal with his mind; he also could kill with a beam from his eyes. He had been able to do that, since he was two.

The ice skinned adolescent had just had enough of the perverted human male lusting after his girlfriend!

Thought became fact, and as the pair walked away down the side road, the truck driver behind could be heard to moan in agony in his sleep; dreaming of his manhood being pinched away, like he was a young bull calf.

He would never again rape another young female.

****

Loni started awake, to find E-ri and Willow standing over them. Like an old man, he gingerly rolled away from his mate, so as not to disturb her, sat up, and rose to his feet.

They moved away from the weary Gem, before they embraced. Willow appeared unharmed; E-ri strong and muscled. These were the children of seven and eight, as they left their world; somehow, now aged to adulthood: thirteen and fourteen.

Loni shook his head, marveling; unable to comprehend immediately.

"You are not well, Poppa," E-ri observed, stepping back. He now stood at an eye level with his foster father.

When did he grow so tall?

"We brought you food, Poppa. You have neglected yourself in tending momma Gem."

Still slow of mind, as if dreaming, the observation caused Loni to turn toward his sleeping partner. Willow had knelt down beside her.

"Has she been sleeping like this the whole time?" the boy questioned, as he handed a foil wrapped hamburger to his father.

Loni dropped to a seated posture, crossing his legs in front; unwrapping the meat in his hands, and taking a huge hungry bite of the succulent patty, before nodding agreement. He hadn't realized he was so ravenous.

How long have I been asleep?

Then realizing why the teen was asking, Loni quickly came to attention.

"Do not try to heal her, E-ri," he objected around an un-chewed mouthful. "Power isn't the same on this world, and...it is also dark...we need to conserve energy."

"I've noticed," E-ri admitted. "Takes a different adjustment. I'm not sure, I even can heal in this world..."

They had been conversing in mind-talk, so as not to awaken the sleeping invalid; even Willow understood the necessity of quiet.

"Has she been eating at all?" queried E-ri, dropping to kneel beside the woman he had called momma since he was two.

Loni shook his head. "Some. But I have rarely dared to leave her to find food..."

"Why is she so...low energy?"

"She was supporting the triune union; the girls were so young to do what they did...and, it took longer than it should. It wasn't instant..."

E-ri nodded, both agreeing, and accepting the logistics of what had happened. Though he couldn't duplicate the same, he understood the mind work it entitled.

"You were doing the same?" he observed.

"We are male; the female has the talent. We support; give energy..."

"I know, Poppa. Believe me..."

"You are different. I don't know why. You have many talents...some only found in females..."

E-ri went silent, neither objecting to the implied praise, nor contradicting his elder.

Loni took another huge bite of his burger.

Golly, but this meat tastes fabulous!

"Where did you get this?" he suddenly asked.

E-ri grinned sheepishly, and the memory of how they came by the food fled through his thoughts. And Loni read every image.

The older man growled deep in his throat, the only verbal sound he could make. It usually signaled profound disapproval.

Then the father realized he could not be the judge. He too had been stealing from the grocery store nearby.

****

Later, when Willow dropped off to sleep, as well, Loni and E-ri stepped to a far corner for a conference. Hunkering down, they squatted, appearing to any outward eye observing, if there had been one, to simply stare at each other, as they silently planned in mental mind-talk.

"This place is unsafe, Poppa," E-ri warned. "We cannot stay here."

"I know," Loni agreed. "But, I simply wasn't strong enough to teleport with her. She can't stay awake long, and isn't physically strong enough to walk far...and...without Gem's knowledge... I do not know how to proceed. This is her world...not mine."

"It's too close to where she was first taken, also," E-ri observed.

Loni nodded. "Overseer settlement...might still be some living near here."

Loni widened his mind. Through E-ri's ears, he was able to distinguish sounds: crickets; the buzzing of flies; mice in the corners, and...dogs baying in the distance; loose and free; hunting.

Dangerous!

Wish I had Lee here.

E-ri read his unguarded thought; nodded in agreement.

"Wonder where the rest are?" Loni added.

"Until Gem is stronger, we will have to stay here. We need to find the others, and...a better, safer hiding place...I noticed you are older..."

E-ri grinned. "A condition acquired in passing..."

"And...do you have the knowledge to go with it?"

"So far...it appears so."

Loni shook his head, awed. E-ri chuckled.

Then the man's thoughts went back to the problem at hand, accepting without further questioning.

"So," Loni finally said. "We will take turns; every other night. You, search for the children; I will seek the elders. I need Brad's expertise...before we move on."

Chapter 9

The nights Loni sat alone, watching the females sleep, guarding them while his son trolled the nearby town and city, the male searched for the mind of the human. This man had once been thought enemy, yet he had become best friend. Loni did not wish to lose him.

Oh, certainly, now that he was back on his home planet, Brad might easily forget them, but Loni hoped that wouldn't be the way it played.

Where would Brad be likely to land? What was the place he would call home. And what of the woman he'd chased the universe to connect with; to reunite and union with again?

Loni had watched him follow her into the portal.

****

Brad had envisioned his home world as he stepped through into the swirling vortex. Jewel was out front, but soon vanished. All Brad could think of, after that, was the graveyard beside which he had spent so many hours grieving the loss of his wife...

So, it was no surprise, that it was where he landed.

And, as he rolled to a jarring stop against her tombstone, his thoughts went to the recovered lost woman, and the relationship they now had.

What area did she picture; what time period was her most pleasant memory? Or...does she remember only the suffering, and pain of those last days here?

****

Jewel, once Lydia, could not suppress a shudder, as she recalled the emotions last experienced on this side; the torturous days just after surgery, when round after round of radiation coupled with chemo destroyed her body; the confusion at the hospital, being unable to communicate, and lastly...the tearing away from her infant, when Brad kept her away.

Oh, yes, she knew, it was for the good of the little one. Radiation; chemo could greatly harm the baby. But the motherly longing was unbearable.

Was it any wonder, the place she arrived was the hospital oncology ward?

Or that...she had forgotten the pleasant times of that other world?

Lydia stood stark naked in the corner of the private room. On the bed to the side, lay a gown, and housecoat, as though waiting to cover her.

Did I have a bath? Why don't they help me to dress?
****

Doctor Harmon was well entrenched in the society of Earth. He'd been here a good while longer than most.

Because, the near pure, Overseer bloodline gave them the resemblance to Egyptian or Eastern Indian males of the planet, it allowed the advance force to infiltrate into the more affluent parts of human society. They had studied the cultures behind these races, their attitudes, and laws. It gave them the ability to blend in well.

Mostly, they took on the roles of physicians, technicians, and politicians; just waiting the chance to take prominent positions. And many had done that over the years. Also, among the human population, were those in policing, or workers on staff in the hospitals all over the well to do areas of the planet. This allowed them liberty to follow up their experiments with treatment; side-lining the patients they chose, disciplining them if they got out of line, and if need be, hiding the more dastardly deeds, should they be necessary.

Harmon was not top Overseer here, but he had his area of control...the Oncology ward of the largest hospital in the city.

He was the first to notice her in the hallway. Seemingly confused; wandering the corridor, as if searching for someone or something...perhaps, a way out. The dark haired woman stood out, because she had hair...on a ward where most were shaved for surgery, or had lost hair due to Chemo treatments.

As he neared, he recognized her:

She had been the companion to the female he had chosen back on his home world. He was second choice behind Doctor Gee; their selection had been found defective, so both males had rejected her. This one, and the other woman, had uncorrectable disorders, making them unfit for reproduction; to be the surrogates to the offspring of an elite physician.

Because of these two women, my dreams of early retirement were dashed!

The two had been scheduled for elimination.

Where did she come from? How is it she still lives?

The domes had blown up! She shouldn't have survived. And how had she gotten here?

He quickly beckoned to a passing nurse. Pointed to the hesitant, errant patient standing uncertain in the middle of the hall.

"Put that woman in isolation...Now!"

Without question, the RN moved immediately to Lydia.

"I do...on't...know...where...I...should...go..." the patient stuttered out with difficulty.

"That's okay, dear." the attendant reassured. "I'll take you..."

As soon as the two were out of sight, Doctor Harmon hurried for his private office.

****

"One of our former subjects, from the home world, is still alive, and has found her way back here. She just turned up on my ward."

"She what?"

"You heard me, What would you like me to do with her?"

"Use your head! Put her down!" the voice on the other end ordered without mercy. "We can't afford disclosure now. It's taken too much to become established in this world. Has she talked to anyone?"

"Rather doubtful. At the moment, she can barely string two words together."

"Good; good." His Superior sounded more calm now. "Consider it priority: eliminate immediately. Oh...and take precautions to make certain there are no others."

"Understood."

Harmon sighed.

What a waste!

****

She was confused; didn't know where she was, but the minute Doctor Harmon entered the room; came to examine her, Lydia knew who he was...and, she remembered.

She couldn't speak well, only stuttered sentences, but Lydia, now Jewel, had learned mind-talk, back in that new world. So, she shouted with all her mind strength, propelling her thoughts into his mind.

And...he couldn't help but understand.

"You stupid booger alien! I know what you are! You are the reason I am like this! You never cared about us; you have no empathy toward us. All you care about is the propagation of your species. That's your only agenda..."

The others with him: nurse and orderlies accompanying him, heard nothing. He heard the words in his head, like a clanging bell.

"You put that thing in my brain; and then you played at your experiments! Because of you, I lost everything...my daughter; my husband; my perfect life here...

"Well, you will pay...someday, you WILL pay! Someday!"

Exhausted, she took a quick breath.

"I know what you do to people in this ward...I know, and...I WILL tell!"

Harmon had come in, still debating with himself. He had thought to set her free; she was helpless; couldn't speak proper; was really no threat. He would choose to disobey the Superior's order; perhaps spirit her away...use her, after all, for himself. But now...she had attacked him, not to mention, she had used mind power. With that forbidden ability, SHE WAS A THREAT!

Anger glowed in his dark soulless eyes. She saw her danger, but didn't care, anymore. This Jewel had been worn thin; her shimmer was gone.

But Lydia/Jewel had no real mind power; no useful defense. She was simply a helpless human being...at his mercy.

"You stupid...booger...on...hu...man...so...ciety..." she stuttered aloud.

The nurse beside him, looked up at the physician in shocked incredulity, her jaw dropping in stunned embarrassment. As she had not heard the former tirade, the spoken word was completely unexpected.

Coldly, doctor Harmon reacted.

"Sedate her," he ordered, quietly.

Lydia reacted accordingly, rolling to the side of the bed, slipping over the edge, and attempting to run. But the orderlies were faster. She struggled valiantly against the two burly men, was soon subdued. The nurse's needle found its mark.

Doctor Harmon turned, and left the room.

Later that evening, when the floor was near empty of attendants, he came into the room, to the sleeping woman. He quietly, indifferently, administered the lethal injection himself, making certain, this time, it was done right.

****

Downstairs, later, many floors below, two turbaned heads were deep in discussion.

"We have sent in hundreds with the Syrian and African migrants. They die by the dozens getting in here, and all that work is for nothing."

"We need to change the speed we infiltrate," Doctor Gee declared. "There is too much build up of new ones in the holding kennels. Those that resemble the Orientals must also be sent out in some fashion. We are overwhelmed!"

"We move those through regular immigration, as family members to the ones already over here in the wealthy communities, but that system is much inundated at present..."

"Surely, the affluent nations will open their big hearts even wider..." Doctor Gee returned with sarcasm.

The other chuckled.

"They have good reason not to. What do our bred changelings do to them for such benevolence?"

Gee grinned maliciously.

"They use to their advantage; over crowd; cause demonstrations, strikes, and riots; they rape, go on mass shootings; and cause overall mayhem..." he answered proudly. "Soon the born to this world will be so overwhelmed, and discouraged, they will give up, and we can completely take over."

The other nodded, agreeing.

"Their generous natures work against them; excellently to our benefit, but...we need to do more. We need to nurture the violent; empty the prisons, and set loose the criminally insane to wreak havoc in the streets. This will serve us more adequately...hurry things up."

"Soon, they will begin to eliminate the elderly; We have done much in this regard. Take the assisted suicide rule. Very beneficial, where we are concerned," Gee revealed. "They already begin to discontinue support for the mentally challenged; set them loose to fend for themselves. We have instigated the cut in benefits to the poorest; food banks are stretched because of it. They are squeezed from all sides."

"The handicapped should be done away with at birth. That would cut their population in half...and give us more access to their funding."

"It is just a matter of changing the mindset, and...the leadership..."

"We have many in governmental positions already," objected his companion.

"True; true, but...they are not nearly enough."

"And, why not? The pace moves according to plan."

A long silence followed, while one waited for the other to speak.

Finally, Gee shook his head, and sighed in desolation.

"I have noted something recently..." He paused, looked about at the other tables in the hospital cafeteria, as though to make certain they would not be overheard.

Most tables were still empty.

"We..." he went on, leaning forward, and speaking in a near whisper. "Are becoming .... inbred. The changed ones are reproducing way too fast..."

"You mean, the white skinned ones?" the other exclaimed incredulously.

"No; no! The dark skins; the ones who look most like us. They are prolific; they copulate like wild beasts; no self-control. Seven, eight, even ten to a family."

"You have paired them?"

"And why not? We have always used the females; now, we simply give many to one male...no different than we did on home planet, but here, we must do it secretly. In this culture, to have many wives is forbidden.

"However...if we don't take over this world soon, completely, as was the original plan; enslave or eliminate all humans...we as a species will pay dearly. As with the home world, there will not be enough room! Our offspring is coming out deformed, sight impaired, and over all, sickly. We have become so inbred, we will cause our own demise! We need their medical facilities to tend to the deficient that are born to us."

"Why do we not simply do as we did in our old world? Put down those unacceptable?"

"And therein lies the problem. The laws here prohibit such behavior, and we cannot change the system fast enough. The beings raised in this civilized culture, the originally born to this world, fight us at every turn. Some could be easily influenced, but..."

"To me, they appear considerably compliant, even naive. We do well..."

Both went silent; suddenly realizing the gravity of the situation.

"How do we do it?" Doctor's Gee's listener demanded, at last. "How do we speed this up?"

"We change the government! The heads hold the power! We have already begun; have a good start..." Gee lowered his voice even further. "The new one here is a good puppet..."

"Ha! Right! The silly 'selfy' prim a donna?"

Gee nodded, approving the choice of words. "And...a second comes on the world stage soon..."

"You refer to the rich one, who alienates and angers all factions?"

"Exactly!"

"Well, then, I fail to see any problem..."

"Ha! It still goes too slow...we need to plan something new; something to rock world opinion, and accelerate our plans. It is that simple."

At that moment, the food court began to rapidly fill up. The two men realized, it was now shift change.

"We will talk more on this matter...later," cautioned Doctor Gee.

"And plan," agreed the other.

Both scraped back their chairs, hurriedly, and rose. Casually, they moved into the milling crowds, as if nothing serious was being discussed. The dark faces, and turbaned heads, easily disguising the tops of their ears, and bristled hair. Soon, they blended in, as if they had never even been there. Yet, what they had revealed would impacted society exceedingly.

Chapter 10

He found her in a back room, all by herself. It was like they had stepped back into the past, to the time just after Lydia's brain surgery.

After many long hours of searching the city streets, Brad had finally thought to try the nearby hospital. By then, it was already night, so he simply walked the quiet halls. No one challenged him; they thought him a visitor waiting on surgery results, or perhaps a family member watching at the bedside of a patient. He had certainly had experience in that department.

His search, at last, paid off, but...by then, it was too late. When he found her, it was evident his Jewel was dying.

She fought for every breath, each gasp more strenuous than the previous one; the labored pants coming shallow at times, other times the wrenching wheeze came from deep down below the diaphragm, as she attempted to get what wasn't available. It was as if, her chest had become paralyzed; or the room around them had gone void, empty of air.

Brad could almost feel her lack of oxygen. Empathy made him dizzy.

He knew it was no point trying to wake her; she would not remember who he was. She could no longer read his mind-talk, nor return his love. What little he read from her mind was confused; she no longer recalled she had a second daughter, or the family she had been a part of on that other world, or...that they had ever been reunited.

Brad checked the chart at the end of the bed. It read 'Jane Doe'; no other details, except...all across the page, diagonally, from corner to opposite corner, huge letters spelled out the sentence, shouted out: DNR (Do not resuscitate).

He knew what that meant. Instinctively, he realized, if he called for help, they wouldn't come, even if there had been someone on the floor at the time.

Brad also knew, this condition was not natural. It had been induced. They had given her something; she had fallen into the hands of the dreaded Overseers, he had heard so much about.

I'm too late...too late. I got here too late to save her.

He climbed up on the bed beside her; lay next to her trembling form; gathered his Jewel in to aching arms. Tears of regret fled hotly down his cheeks, as he hugged her close.

Whatever will I do without you?

If only he could teleport like the telepaths. If only Loni and Gem were here. But no, they were on their own. They were all alone, back in a hateful, uncaring world.

Why? Why us? What did we ever do to you?

He felt her spasm, in a last hopeless effort to hang on to elusive life. Brad experienced it; her soul escaping the fragile being, that had once been the love of his life.

He waited; it seemed like hours, but was merely...seconds. They went by snail slow, painfully. No other breath followed.

The minutes ticked by; room so dead silent...like a tomb.

Dead. Yes. Jewel is dead.

He had found her, only to lose her again.

Brad lay by her side through most of that night. He grieved, alone, silently, afraid to cry out his anger, his anguish, for fear they might hear, and take her away.

What will I tell Willow? And what about...poor little Nitha?

Where the hell are the others, anyway?

He sat beside her stiff cold body, his back toward her, head in his hands. Desperate; feeling hopeless.

Toward shift change, around seven-thirty, Brad heard footsteps approaching. Suddenly, he was panicked.

Have to hide!

One part of him wanted to lie beside his lover, be caught, and die, as well.

Let them do their worst to me!

The other side knew, he must survive...to avenge this exquisite personality they had just murdered.

Someday...someday!

He had to flee! To hide. He gazed about the sparse room...the unlit bathroom, its door slightly ajar.

Brad quickly kissed the cooling cheek of his dead wife, then jumped away from her, off the bed. He barely made it across the room, and inside the darkened space...

An orderly entered the room beyond, just as Brad slid the door to the restroom closed, to sit, holding his breath, on the cold, white stool...waiting.

The dark burly man inside checked the still patient. Quickly, left the room, again.

Brad waited. He knew it was too soon to leave. He would be discovered for certain.

Minutes later, hurried steps; two pairs of feet. A nurse was with the blue clad man this time. A whispered conference. The man left; the woman remained.

The orderly returned pushing a stretcher. Together, the pair loaded the empty shell from the bed, covered it with a sheet, and wheeled it toward the door.

Brad wanted to yell at them, to order them to leave her be, but no...

He dare not. Nor could he follow, when they took her away.

****

Gem awoke with a start. Willow lay beside her; E-ri was propped against the naked ribs of the barn wall behind them, dozing. Loni was missing, but she knew, instinctively, he was out seeking; out in the night somewhere, looking for Jewel and Brad.

Jewel. That's what woke me. The dream...

But it hadn't been a dream.

Gem sighed, disheartened.

E-ri opened his eyes. He had dreamed the nightmare, too.

"Jewel...is no more," Gem stated bluntly in mind-talk. The grief near overcame her, but she quickly mastered it. Jewel had been a good friend; a female confidant. She would be deeply missed.

E-ri nodded.

Like Gem; as with all telepaths, in varying degrees, he had the same ability for precognition. They knew things, sensed them before, and as, they happened. All that was needed was a familiarity with the person, and this subject was close to them both, had been since the boy had been infant.

Loni came visible in the middle of the huge, dilapidated, gutted structure. His sense of happening, sending him to check on those he knew would struggle with this.

"Ah," he stated in quiet mind-talk. "You have finally awakened." And then at her sad countenance, he added: "I know. She is gone..."

"Brad will be devastated..."

"Brad IS devastated!" Loni agreed.

All three ice-blue beings turned their eyes to the sleeping golden skinned, dark haired girl on the straw.

Willow.

The word went through each mind accompanied by the feelings of sympathy, sorrow, fondness; helpless grief for her. Rarely did the telepaths converse between themselves, other than in mind-talk, so the thirteen year old girl had remained in slumber.

"We will need to tell her...her mother is...gone," Gem decided.

E-ri appeared near to tears; both his empathy, and anger, showing boldly. "Let me, momma," he offered.

"Gently," Gem cautioned, then turned to her mate.

"Will you fetch Brad?"

Loni shook his head. "Not just yet. He'll need time to process, and...grieve."

"The Opposites know we are back here, now," Gem warned. "They will be watching for us. Be careful, when you do go."

****

"How old, approximately, would you say this male is?" enquired Doctor Gee of the orderly standing before the council.

The man made a face, screwing up his nose, with the effort to think out his answer. Finally, he gave his hesitant reply: "He was...perhaps in his forties. I am not much of a judge as to their ages..."

"Color of skin?"

"Caucasian..."

Gee nodded. He knew, who they were dealing with before they investigated.

"Okay," he decided. "We will deal with it from here."

When his attendant had left the room, Gee turned to Doctor Harmon, and the others with him.

"He will not have left the city just yet," he declared. "But, we must work fast..."

"Why would he not have left, yet?" questioned one of the others.

"This male," Doctor Harmon answered for his leader. "Is the original partner to the female I just put down. We should have eliminated him from the first! Because we didn't..." At a warning look from Gee, he kept the rest of his thoughts to himself. Added: "He has a long history of searching for her..."

"And, we know for certain, it was he, that was seen in the halls?"

"Yes. Identification is verified from surveillance cameras," agreed a third.

"He already has a grave site for her; buried her once before," Harmon went on. "It is within the city limits. When he cannot find her body, he will, no doubt, go there to mourn her..."

"What have we done with the body, now?"

"It was quickly cremated. No more trouble that way."

"This is what we will do with HIM," Gee abruptly interrupted, to prevent further side tracking.

He turned to the man beside him, instructing: "Tweak the compound to target all males over thirty..."

Another interrupted, annoyed: "How do we administer it, when we cannot even get close to him?"

"If you will be patient!" Gee grumbled. "I was about to tell you! We put it into the city's water supply..."

"But won't that target all beings in the city? Just for this one male! Is it worth it?"

"This male is deadly to our cause! He has been with this female; someway, he lost her...at least, that is what we assume. They somehow, must have gotten together, and came together through an open portal. Anyway, she would have told him much..."

"But," objected another. "I thought you said, she could no longer verbalize?"

Harmon cleared his throat for attention. All eyes turned toward him.

"She," he admitted, ominously. "Has learned the dreaded...mind-talk..."

Each person present drew in a shocked breath.

"So, you see, his demise is essential..."

"Is he...able, also, to...mind-talk?"

"Most likely," Harmon stated, tersely.

"Continue, then," agreed one of the listeners, of Doctor Gee. "How do you intend to deal with this?"

"At some point, he must surely drink coffee, or some other prepared beverage," Gee carried on. "All he needs to swallow is one dose..."

"How long will it take to enter the water system?"

"Seventy-two hours, and it will be in every building, and water tap."

"And how long to flush back out into the river?"

"A month."

"So..." pondered another. "We may lose some of our own?"

"We will pass the word to drink bottled water. If any are too stupid to obey the edit, they deserve to die."

"And how exactly does the compound present?"

"It mimics dysentery. All males over thirty, who drink it will die in convulsions within six hours."

"So immediately lethal? You have managed to fine tune the virus to that extent?"

Gee nodded gravely.

"This will not target the females, will it?" asked another.

"It attacks the male chromosome only."

"Excellent! That actually benefits us in two ways..."

A second agreed. "The fighting men, and older, wiser males in the population will be exterminated. Ha! We should set this lose all across the planet, not just here in one city."

"That would settle a lot of our problems," agreed a third. "Then, if we sterilize the younger males as they are born..."

Harmon had sat listening, annoyed by their lack of vision. He interjected some much needed reality to the conversation.

"Never underestimate the females," he declared, forcefully. "If they have an inkling of what we do, they will fight us as violently as any male. Another thing we need to consider: we need some males to remain in population, to blame, and...lead for us."

"Ah, yes," Gee agreed. "We can always blame ISIS..."

"For this?" Another laughed. "They will eventually discover the water as the source..."

"Most certainly," agreed a second. "They will put out a water advisory...after some delay..."

"As you well know, from past experience, that will take them weeks, even more, until something is actually done," Harmon interjected.

"And," Gee put in. " By that time, it will have flushed from the system, and our target will have died a most excruciating death."

Chapter 11

It seemed E-ri always felt angry, now. Tonight, he had reluctantly went out in search of his missing sisters. leaving Willow to grieve on her own, not just because she needed the alone time to process, but also, unable to console her, because he, himself, was in such a sulk.

Being a teen sucks!

He had always wanted to be older, but now that he was actually fourteen, the novelty was fast wearing thin. It meant, he must always be responsible for his actions, to perform as though, grown up.

Yes, he had done that most of his life, but now that it was required, the process had actually become, painful. E-ri longed for his lost childhood, which he had forfeited by continuously playing guardian.

What had touched this unpleasant mood off in him was, as he comforted Willow, he had dropped his mind guard protection, and Loni had read what he did not want him to see: that E-ri had retaliated, and done harm to another; something Loni had taught all his children, from infancy, was wrong; forbidden. Loni had discovered, E-ri had mutilated the human truck driver. And worse than that, E-ri had read the man's past memories; his crimes against women and young girls.

Loni and Gem had drilled it into the young ones they raised, from the very beginning: 'Privacy is vital! Never invade the musing of another; especially, not their memories...unless it is offered.'

'Most of all; Never harm! Never kill!'

For the first time in his young life, E-ri had been reprimanded; scolded. Stiffly!

And no chastising ever sits well in a developing adult.

E-ri felt bruised. Unloved. Yet, a part of him knew; his foster parent was right...somewhat. With the powers he possessed, guidelines were needed.

Still, E-ri needed to sort it all out.

Loni also had taught the boy self-control; if that had not taken root, the world about him would be exploding, at this point. To wear off the frustration he was feeling, E-ri had gone out prowling.

Besides, he needed to find the missing females...

Yet the area he walked in, did little to improve his mood.

As he followed the surface thoughts of the trolling clientele; their lust, violence, and perversion drove his mind ballistic. At this time of night, the streets reeked of it.

He pictured his foster sisters trapped in the situations of this neighborhood...Nitha in the hands of a prostitution ring; in some dive, being roughed up, or ravished by a man twice her size. And Thea...

Thea was most like a sister to E-ri; he could never bear what they might do to her...

Yet, it was she, he found first.
****

As the first shades of a new dawn was painting the horizon, E-ri finally got a sense of the essence of his sister. He followed it with excited anticipation, to the utter most edge of the city limits.

On the far side of the huge garbage dump, beneath piles of bulging black, or green, plastic bags, in stark contrast against them, E-ri found Thea. He could not have missed the body.

It was as white as the paper sheets swirling about in the putrid wind; no longer was she breathing; her spirit barely present in its broken shell.

The battered pale body was streaked with bright red blood; the face pushed in from more than one blow; the limbs blue and black, twisted in shapes unnatural.

He cried out in wrathful rejection at what he saw; knew immediately, this was not the work of Overseers.

No! This is human done!

The Overseer mind set had spread like a plague.

E-ri knew it was pointless to try to heal his foster sister out here in the open...even if he, a male could, for it was best for female to heal female.

He gathered her naked body in his arms, and jumped to the broken down barn, where the few he knew were safely rescued.

Gem and Willow greeted him with grief in their eyes, knowing by foreknowledge what he had discovered.

Loni, who seldom spoke aloud, gave an outraged cry at sight of his daughter, and seemed to melt into a forlorn, dejected creature.

"Loni! Poppa! I need you to pull it together!" E-ri commanded. "I need your help!"

"She's female! E-ri. She's female...without a mate! A male can't heal her!" Loni shouted back in mind-talk, beside himself, thinking E-ri wanted him to do the healing.

They both knew, Gem was still too weak to do a full outright healing.

For a moment Loni stood there, tears in his eyes; his gaze went to the mother of his child. Gem also appeared uncertain what to do, rooted to the spot.

"I will try... For now, we will make her comfortable."

With that, Loni came back to his ordered self. He stepped forward, arms extended to take Thea from E-ri. But the boy refused to relinquish his sister.

He moved to the sleeping place, they had prepared for Gem; tenderly, carefully, he lay his burden on the straw. When E-ri stepped back, he exploded; his adulthood lost; the small boy returned; all that was now left.

"I HATE HUMANS!" he growled aloud, with venom. "I HATE THEM ALL!"

Willow moved quietly forward; attempted to wrap him in her arms. E-ri stepped back, not desiring comfort just yet; angry; belligerent.

"Me, too? Even me?" she probed, relentlessly.

E-ri looked down at her, his face dissolving into hurt; his lip quivering. She moved forward again, and surrounded him in her arms.

E-ri went limp, giving way to tears.

****

All through that day, and most of the next, as she was able, Gem worked on the healing of her ice-skinned daughter. Only because there was still essence within the broken shell, was it even possible.

But, only by degrees, a limb at a time; a bruised organ; carefully; excruciatingly...and Gem, not fully recovered herself, took a long time healing back. There was much waiting between.

****

E-ri had found a small cell phone. With adjustments, Loni was able to gain access to the internet. They could listen, and sometimes even see, news broadcasts.

It was weeks later, when deadly information came to them, via this damaged instrument...

'...It targets those over thirty; most dying are men. Again, we warn you; do not drink the water! We do not believe the virus airborne, and it was discovered in the water system of only one major city, but, could easily spread, as it has now passed into the river system...' At that point the announcer faded out, but all in the barn understood the implication to them.

When no more sound was forth coming, Loni turn the device off.

E-ri moaned aloud. "I did this; this is my fault! I was the one cursed humans..."

"No!" Loni declared in mind-talk, his voice adamant. "The Opposites have done this. It is meant to flush out Brad! In our own tragedy, I have forgotten all about him..."

"He will likely be dead by now..."

"No, son...we...I would feel...his end."

Chapter 12

Brad sat desolate, beside the tombstone, in the landscaped graveyard. He knew nowhere else to go. He had tried to follow after the intern, wheeling away his wife, but he had soon lost him. Later, after asking questions, he had found the morgue freezer, but before he had found a way to spirit away the body, they had sent her out in a van, to be cremated. Brad knew, he would never she her remains again.

So, this was where he had come...to get even remotely close to her, where he had buried an empty container, he'd been given, the first time.

But, he stewed at the circumstances that had brought him to this point.

It was here, he had thought his beloved gone to rest, all those many years before, but never once, had he believed her dead. They had never found a body!

That was why he had joined the searchers, beneath the ocean, who had scavenged the wreckage of the plane, and how he had come upon the portal, beneath the undersea hill.

And...how, he had come into Azure Blue.

All his adventures; the tribulations endured...it seemed so dream-like now. If it hadn't been for those vague memories, of Jewel and his girls; of Loni and Gem, and their motley crew, Brad might reason, he was the demonic from the bible, so mad, that he lived here among the tombstones.

What is the point? Lydia is no more. I found my lost wife, only to lose her again.

But...he did remember Gem's clear order: 'We have to step into the portal, manually. Go! Hurry! Go! Go!'

But where are the others?

He also remembered those blood thirsty soldiers who had invaded that other world, just when he was adjusting so nicely to his new life.

As if from long habit, he patted his hip, like there should be pockets there, as he had in his hide shorts, back on Azure Blue. He caught himself, and sighed.

He had lost those while in transit through the portal; come through naked, then pilfered shorts and a sleeveless tank top, from a clothes line along the way.

Later, at the hospital, he had traded those for scrubs and booties, to blend in. But, the scrub pants had no pockets, and that meant...he had no money.

No money! Yeah, and I am back on Earth...where you can do nothing without some means of currency, or trade. Nothing is free here! What am I going to do?

Well...first order of business...something to eat, and...

Gazing around him, Brad spied a raised, abandoned casket, sitting on rails. It was obvious, that funeral was over. The coffin was dirty, as if it had been lowered, dirt shoveled in, for the benefit of the mourners, then raised, once more, after they had gone.

Perhaps, here is a source...something? Some people believe the dead need things on the other side...

Oh, brother. I'm about to rob a dead man!

Well, he sure won't need what he's wearing! And I need another disguise? They know what I am wearing, and they'll be darn sure hunting me.

It was just growing light. Slinking forward, Brad crept to the casket. With some effort, he managed to open the lid. But, when he lifted it, the body inside was female, not male.

Oh, well... I can go transvestite? Or...as a street tramp...

But now, he had another problem. The elderly matriarch was excessively obese. At least, she was wearing a suit...with pants.

She also had on expensive jewelry...which helped. It could be pawned.

He made quick work of changing from the scrubs, and booties.

Brad wasn't able to use the old woman's shoes, so he went bare foot. He knew, he couldn't walk the streets with no shoes, for long. It had been hard enough getting to the grave site.

Today, it was cold; the paved road was rough, and freezing.

****

It was mid-day, by the time he had returned to the city limits. The hospital had been at the edge of the city, easy enough to pass through the few streets to the graveyard, but going back...it was a much longer route to city center, where the shops were. The soles of his feet were soon raw.

He easily found an open pawn shop. The clerk looked up at him, askance; with his trousers rolled up, so he wouldn't trip, and the over-sized jacket, so big, he swam in it. He had kept the tank top on beneath, so he had merely buttoned the top button on the coat. It hung loose and baggy.

Two of the soldiers, back on Azure Blue, had roughed him up good, but that had been days ago. You would have thought, after going through a time portal, those injuries would have healed some. But, no; here he was sporting a bruised, puffy face, as well.

The shop owner finally shrugged, as if his appearance was something he was used to, and accepted the fact, Brad needed money. But...he would give little for the broach, ring, and earrings.

They merely netted Brad, fifty bucks. In this overpriced, driven economy, that wouldn't last long.

I have to stay out of sight, anyway...can't stay in a hotel.

As Brad sat at a table, outside the fast food diner, eating, ready to run at the least provocation, he thought on his next move...a job.

Man! These fries taste good. Can't wait to bite into that burger...should have gotten root beer; not just bottled water...

His thoughts returned to the problem at hand.

He was well muscled, though still favoring his injured hip. He could lift; he had been swinging through trees, back in that other world...

But, my appearance will turn off most employers...

****

Every time another job prospect fell through; every night, Brad returned to the grave site of his lover. Then, for many days, he would grieve again, for Jewel...he no longer thought of her as Lydia. And, for his missing girls.

Should be looking for them...

But, he stood out so badly, looking for a job...

What is the point?

He grieved, silently, and alone, as if all three were dead. Depressed; without hope.

Until...

One night, against the pitch dark of an obsidian sky, Brad saw the glowing shape of an ice-blue alien.

Seething with anger, Brad bolted up. He ran straight at the slight form. For long seconds, he pummeled him viciously with his fists.

Loni made no effort to fight back.

Finally, his wrath spent, Brad stepped back, and shouted verbally at his mentor.

"Where were you? When I needed you! They killed her! The Overseers MURDERED Jewel!"

Brad had thought the wells of grief were emptied, but when his friend reached out to embrace him, he slumped into Loni's arms, and the flood gates opened as from a waterfall.

Brad sank to his knees sobbing like an abandoned child. Loni simply held him, rubbing his back for comfort.

Chapter 13

They still took turns patrolling at night. Brad had settled in; he stayed with the females while the blue skinned males went seeking the missing children; Loni went one way; E-ri the other. Then, in daylight, Brad walked the streets, as well.

He was now clothed more presentably.

This night E-ri had gone out alone. The two grown men had things to discuss.

Also, tonight E-ri had picked up an essence, though very faint...of Nitha.

But, as is often the case, in this predatory world; with anyone different; E-ri had become a target, as well. With his glowing form, he stood out against the dark sky, even in the lighted streets he traversed. Soon, he attracted the malevolent attention of a gang: three oversized bullies, and one younger boy, with the intention of impressing his older companions.

E-ri felt Nitha's pain; sensed her bewildered mind. Just as he was about to go invisible, and enter the motel, his concentration was broken; the essence faded away to nothingness.

He had been concentrating so hard, he was unaware, as the thugs came from behind. They had him surrounded, before he realized, he was in danger.

The first E-ri knew, before he could turn, they were at him with iron bars; knives, and lethal feet, tripping him. E-ri stumbled, as a heavy male mounted his back; clung to his shoulders; soon had an arm around his neck in a choke hold.

E-ri danced about, attempting to shake the teen loose; his rider swinging at his head with something in his fist. E-ri couldn't see what he held. Something metal, and extremely hard, crashed against his skull. The black night turned to grey, before his eyes, and E-ri drifted away; knew nothing more.

****

Gee slammed the door with unnecessary force, as he entered his lavish home. He was fuming mad.

Things had not gone well this day; it had been long and hard; more difficult than usual; beyond endurance...to keep that soft look of compassion on his face; a tone of understanding in his voice. Just so they would not realize the hatred he felt toward them.

Patients! I'd like to torture them all. Slowly! Always complaining...as if I could actually ease their pain. As if, I would want to!

He needed to vent!

He didn't have to shout out for a female; the violent way he had entered sent the clues; they knew what to do. And...silently, the dark skinned maiden was by his side, eager to serve.

It didn't matter that this one was one of his own grown daughters...

He would have taken her down upon the bare hardwood floor. But for his own comfort, he chose the sofa; in his mad lust frenzy, stripping, and ripping, roughly, at the silken garment she wore. Violently, he entered the soft rear between the cheeks. She made no outcry.

She wouldn't dare!

After the initial thrust, and release, he sank beside her, spent. Moments later, he eased back, turned the girl about, and encouraged her to continue normal massage, to arouse himself again.

Once is too little.

But, his thoughts were still on the one wrathful fact that had driven him to this point:

Somehow, that white human male had eluded their trap. And, he no longer came to the empty grave site of his wife...nor could he be found among the sick in the ERs; the dead in the morgue; or anywhere on the streets.

This meant, they had to call off the hunt. They simply didn't have the manpower.

And...the lab had just told him, the virus was no longer viable!

He stewed over this, while his daughter attempted to please him. What Doctor Gee did not know, was that this very daughter had recently been down by the river; had bathed in its waters, before coming home.

Nor did he realize, the virus upon hitting that river system, had mutated, to exclusively attack the original donors of the DNA strain used to develop it.

As the beautiful girl fondled him, her touch became lethal; turning the tables. Predator became prey...

Gee suddenly stiffened. The young girl sprang screaming from the couch, as her father went into convulsions. He died within minutes, frothing at the mouth.

****

E-ri slowly came to awareness. Three of the bullies were still kicking him, the fourth had his arm twisted at his back. His attacker yanked hard on the arm, pulling it toward E-ri's opposite shoulder. E-ri felt the searing pain, but did not hear the crunching crack. He went under again...

When vision returned, E-ri was laying sprawled on his back, his right arm useless, feeling bruised, and battered. If his mind and eyes would work, he just might have a chance. But, it was night; energy depleted.

Above him, he saw the leader of the pack kneeling at his side, a knife in his hand. Behind, his fellow antagonists stood gawking, laughing, and egging him on.

To E-ri, the next string of events, appeared as in a foggy dream sequence:

Out of the darkness, came a giant black bird. Its face appeared gargoyle-like; the dark wing span, at least twelve feet across, from one side to the other; man-like black torso; hands and arms; feet with toes...

Was it wearing, shorts?

Swooping like a giant black monster, the apparition first picked up the skinny younger boy at the back. It tossed him hard, against the brick wall of a building on the left. The victim bounced back from the blow; wind knocked out of him; slid down the wall; unconscious.

Next, the second and third beefy observers, followed this younger one, tossed away like pieces of a toy army, no longer entertaining to the child at play. As each was removed, only the attacker with the knife remained bent over E-ri.

Just as this man, drove his knife down toward the chest of the ice-skinned boy, the thing...landed behind them, and caught the assailant by the throat. Hand opened by reflex; the weapon dropped, landing with a bounce, skittering off somewhere, beneath a huge dumpster box.

Then, the dark creature rose into the air, the native male, in his grasp, still struggling frantically, at the hands about his neck, swinging, feet pumping, desperately trying to force release.

In fear, E-ri closed his eyes. Thinking he was next, he raised a mental/physical barrier, like a transparent visible bubble, as a shield around himself.

It took him a moment to realize he was suddenly alone.

When he finally did look around, E-ri first noticed three of his attackers, all senseless against a far wall. Being on the ground, he automatically looked skyward. The sight that met his eyes made him draw in a shocked, quick breath.

Still suspended in the arms of the man-like bird, the native bully had gone limp. From extremely high up, as the dark hands let go, his would-be killer plunged to the pavement of the alley.

For a moment, the black creature hovered. Then, slowly folding its wings, it eased down, to stand in the dirty alley beside E-ri's prostrate form.

"Are you much hurt, E-ri?"

To the blue-skinned boy's utter shock, the voice in his head spoke mind-talk. It was then, he recognized his rescuer.

"Peek?"

This did not look at all like his boyhood friend. In contrast to the glowing ice-blue boy, Peek's skin was a chocolate black/brown, the body, that of a skinny twelve year old; long stringy, dreadlock braids; but still, the face of Peek, with one side slack, the lip, as well, in a perpetually unhappy downturn; the eye lid on that side, half closed. He appeared to be half starved, his belly touching his backbone.

E-ri dropped his defensive shield.

"Peek!"

In spite of his aching, useless arm; his quickly blackening bruises, he leapt to his feet, and enfolded the other boy in a bone-crunching, one armed hug.

"Oh, easy, bro," Peek moaned. "Not so...tight...you'll break me."

E-ri stepped back, chuckling.

"How?" he demanded. "Where have you been?"

"First, we need to get away from here..."

E-ri nodded agreement. The conversation had been in mind-talk; silent. It was so good to finally be able to converse in a normal way, with someone from home world.

"Can you walk?" asked Peek, as he scanned the bruised body of his childhood friend. "I don't think I can fly us both for very long..."

"You have wings," E-ri marveled, grinning.

Peek smiled sheepishly, and apologetically defended, with a shrug. "New development..."

Just before Peek could shield his inner memories, E-ri read some of the horror the other boy had lived through, during the time they had been separated.

"Maybe, I can jump us in segments..."

Chapter 14

"We can't simply continue to steal as we do?" Brad declared. "Eventually, one of us is going to get caught..."

"We cannot integrate into their society. It is obvious, they will never let us!" Loni declared, vehemently. "Our own appearance stands against us..."

"And now, you say, Overseers are taking over this world." Brad shook his head. "They already hunt me... Whatever are we to do?"

"We need to find a safe haven, as we had on the other world..." Gem suggested.

"Oh, there is no safe haven, here! Human soldiers will be looking for us..." Brad objected. "That is, if some came through after us..."

"Be assured. They did!" Gem agreed. "It won't be long until they find us..."

"Are we to leave this world to the Overseers? Not even challenge them?" objected Loni.

"It appears their presence is satisfactory to those born here..."

Loni made a rude noise. "You were born here, Gem!"

"So was Willow," agreed Brad.

"And you..." Gem quietly added. "We all agree, the Overseers should not rule here! But...at the moment, you, Brad, are our best asset; our only hope. We can do little about Overseer activity. No more than we could back on Azure Blue. We need to make a safe haven," she repeated. "Then, from there we can do...whatever is possible..."

"We are older, now; not as strong, " objected Loni. "Our powers don't work the same here..."

"And..." Brad cut in. "We don't have free reign, as we did on Azure Blue. Do you realize? We need to BUY supplies; food...put up barriers for safety. We don't even have property! We need to own a piece of property, where no one will bother us."

Moaning aloud, Brad dropped his head in his hands. Moments later, he raised his eyes to the other two, and tried to explain, what he knew, Loni didn't understand.

"Because my appearance is human, I am the only one who can go out in public....but, I have been declared dead. Without the proper identification cards, I can't even legally work! Oh, yes, under the table, I can be paid in cash, but you don't want to deal with the people who do that..."

Both Loni and Gem read the images that went through his mind. Loni frowned; Gem gave a shiver.

"It won't take long, and I'll come up against the law...and, then there is the Overseers; they know my face....

"I can't buy or sell...anything! And nothing on this world is free! Especially, here in, what they call, the 'civilized' world."

Gem nodded in agreement; backed him up.

"No money; no documents. This society; this side of the world, runs by strict rules of engagement. Even were Loni, E-ri, Thea, and I in disguise, we could not be hired without some form of identification..."

"You can't even buy food without money," Brad put in. "Rarely do they barter."

Loni shook his head, disbelieving such a culture could exist.

"Is it greed? Is that what propels it?"

"Afraid so," Brad returned with shame.

"I cannot understand why this planet is so...venerated. Why don't you change things?"

"Why did you not stop the Overseers in your world?"

"We were powerless...or didn't know any different..." Suddenly, Loni understood.

"There ARE ways around this," Gem finally cut in. "We need to find a remote area; a piece of property useless to others. That's where we begin. Plow the field; steal seeds...if we must. Start our own garden..."

"Yes!" Brad exclaimed. "While in the city, at the library, I got on the free internet connection, and checked on available remote property. I found many that have been abandoned for years...I printed out a few..."

He dug into the old knap sack, he had acquired along the way. It had been tossed aside by some errant school boy; Brad found the bag, soaking wet, under bushes; dried it out, and now, carried it with him where ever he went.

Through Brad's eyes, Loni and his sightless companion scanned the pages with him.

"Here's one that would be perfect." Brad spread it out. "It's way up north by a lake..."

Gem's hand sought the bottom of the page. Brad's eyes quickly followed so she could see.

"See closer," Gem ordered.

He pulled the sheet within inches of his eyes; read the name of the seller, realtor, and sales person.

At Gem's quick intake of breath, Loni demanded: "What?"

"That's my SISTER!" exploded in their minds.

"Yeah..." Brad hated to burst their bubble. "But...we still have no way to buy it."

Gem let out an exasperated sigh.

* * * *

While the men continued in discussion, Gem sat thinking.

They had simply dismissed the fact her sister was the realtor's representative...

Bella...my sister!

But it had been seven years, since they had even seen each other. A lot had happened...

Through mind suggestion, a human can be easily made to do things...

Wonder what she did with my things?

"I can't get a loan, Loni!" Brad insisted heatedly. "We can't buy the piece of property without a loan...or cash. That's a lot of cash. I can't get that much, unless...I steal it. And then, if we use it to buy something this large, the police will be all over us..."

"Minds can be manipulated..." Loni suggested, slowly. "They can be made to think it's been paid..."

"Paper work needs to back possession. Can you get that filled out, so no one knows what's been done?"

Loni shook his head despondently, and sighed.

"I may have a solution," Gem broke in cautiously. "I can go to my sister..."

"Oh, no, you don't!" Loni objected immediately, his mental tone indignant. "That woman abandoned you! When you needed help in treatment, she just left you to fend for yourself!"

"I know, Loni," Gem agreed. "But, I need to make peace. Forgive her..."

Loni growled angrily, deep in his throat; the only sound he could make. He often used it to make known just how deeply he disagreed. His mate shook her head in warning.

"Loni, don't judge. We don't know what she might have been going through at the time. I have no idea her reasons, and...maybe, she has changed. It's worth a try. She could help me get established again."

Loni relaxed, pondering on the suggestion.

"You would need to go in disguise," he finally agreed, with mind talk. "Heavily made up, to hide your skin color, and cover your eyes." Gem sighed, but nodded. "And no going alone..."

"I have to go alone," objected Gem. "Please, let me do this..."

Before Loni could answer her, an ear splitting scream split the silence. Willow sat up on her bed of straw, her cry waking Thea, as well. Their discussion came to an abrupt halt.

Chapter 15

Willow woke with a start, the scream still on her lips, her barely remembered nightmare still clawing at the edges of her mind. Beside her, Thea sat bolt upright, as if she too had been a part of the dream.

The two had been peacefully slumbering, side-by-side, while the adults were in earnest debate.

Across from the girls, stood the hay loft, a platform twelve feet above the floor. The double doors to the outside stood open to the charcoal sky, stars winking in the distance.

When Willow opened her eyes, the first thing she saw, was E-ri swinging suspended, against this back drop; limp, battered, broken, and unconscious, in the arms of, what appeared to be, a huge, hideous, black-winged creature, hovering above the platform.

The monster swooped in; landed with an ungraceful stumble, as if his load were too heavy; fell forward over E-ri; the dark body, and gossamer wings drooping; going limp, like crepe paper wrapping, laid out over E-ri, as if to hide him.

Willow screamed a second time. To her, it appeared, as if her dream had become reality.

Brad sprang up, making for the loft; Loni followed, ready to defend. Thea enfolded her friend in a compassionate hold.

Gem suddenly yelled: "Stop!"

Their minds filled with visions, so fast it was difficult to follow. Yet, these were not warnings; mere pictures of a past, and the boys lying there.

"That is no enemy! It's Peek...with E-ri!"

Soon everyone had climbed the ladder to the loft, surrounded the pair of prone forms on the scattered straw.

The voice in their minds came from the dark one on top.

"I couldn't hold him any longer...E-ri was hurt, couldn't teleport us any further, so...I tried to fly us the rest of the way..."

The gigantic wings slowly folded away, disappearing into the deformed bone structure of shoulders and back. Peek sighed, and rolled over, gasping out words, aloud.

"Sorry, I scared you. E-ri was attacked by a gang. They beat him..."

There was no farther need to explain. Loni was kneeling at E-ri's side, immediately, beginning his healing.

****

Willow was enthralled by Peek's new wings. Up close, his misshapen face didn't faze her; she had seen that back on Azure Blue: the sagging cheek; the half-closed eye; the crooked grin, one side wilting, as if refusing to follow the other.

To others, he might look like one of those gargoyles, she had seen so often on TV and in books...especially, when he hunched over, and spread those big wings to show off. But, to her, he was only another protective brother...

Oh, but what wings! Black feathers, almost like leather, with a sliver sheen to them, when the moon light hit the tips of them. Their span must be, at least, twelve feet from side to side.

And, he hides all that, folded away behind his shoulder blades...

With constant use, over the miles he had flown to get to them, they had developed stronger; larger with each day; his chest muscles bulging, rippled with power.

When he stood before you, without his wings expanded, covered by a shirt, he might look small, but...the minute the wings spread, Peek became a formidable monster.

A mere boy...only twelve; small for that age...he had always been diminutive... Now, their hidden weapon.

He could sit on a roof at night, and never be seen or noticed...

Chapter 16

Her boyfriend had gone out, finally, leaving her alone. Bella wasn't sure she even wanted him staying with her. He was so controlling; complicated her life terribly.

He had disappeared seven years ago, just dropped off the face of the earth. She had thought he might be dead. At the time, so much had been going on in her life, with the loss of her sister, and all, she had almost been relieved, that he had vanished from sight.

But, here he was back once more, expecting their relationship to pick up where it had left off. He was more violent now, more quick tempered.

He had killed her beautiful puppy, the first day he'd been here. She knew it was useless to pursue any demand for retribution; there would be hell to pay, if she did.

It made Bella cringe; the thought of what he might do next.

But, she was unsure, how to expel him from her life.

Just in case, and to be careful, so she wouldn't come up against his wrath, again, she had left the side door open, so her man could get back in, but she knew, when he took off like this, he seldom returned the same day. It might be a week, months, or even a year, before he turned up again.

Bella had just finished washing up her few dishes; walked into the open space she called living room, to sit down. What she did not expect, was to find an elderly woman standing there, uncertain, just inside the door.

"Well!" Bella declared indignantly. "You could at least knock, before coming in."

"Bella..." The hesitant, soft voice was familiar, but Bella couldn't place it. "I'm...your sister. Gemma?"

Bella shot back with a quick, curt reply.

"My sister is dead! Died over seven years ago...in a plane crash. But, no doubt, you know that, don't you?"

"I AM your sister," the old woman quietly insisted.

"Prove it!"

"We had a little black lab puppy when we were small. We called her 'Lucky', but she was far from lucky, got hit by a transit bus, as it was coming down the hill. Lucky had followed an older golden lab across the highway. The big one got across, but our puppy was caught by the front end of the bus. She was hurt too bad; we had to put her down."

Bella sucked in her breath, as memory hit. For long moments, she went silent.

"How old were we?" she finally fired back.

"Three and four."

"And...who is older? You or me?"

"You are..."

"Humph!" she grunted. "You sure don't look like my sister Gemma. Where you been all this time? Well...come on in. No use standing there. You want some tea?"

"Ah...no, thank you. I can't stay long..."

When the pair were seated across from each other, Bella took note of the woman more closely. She appeared sickly; her skin very pale, almost a bluish-white tint. Gemma had covered her white hair with a kerchief, wore dark glasses, as if she didn't want to be noticed. She was dressed in baggy farmer's coveralls, half hidden by an oversized padded jacket.

Dressed way too heavy for such a warm day.

And, until now, Bella hadn't realized, she was in stocking feet.

"Where are your shoes?"

"Haven't any."

"Are you in trouble?"

Gemma shook her head.

Bella harrumphed a second time.

"I suppose you expect me to take you in?" When no answer appeared to be forthcoming, Bella went on. "I can barely make my own bills," she declared indignantly. "Sure can't take care of you. I had to pay for your funeral, you know, and here, you aren't even dead. You cleaned out your bank account before you disappeared..."

"What funeral?"

"They finally declared you dead. I had to have some kind of memorial..."

"Anybody come?"

Bella gave a rude grunt, meant to be sarcastic. "Why should they? I spent that money for nothing!"

"Sorry..."

"Ya. Now, you're sorry. Come crawling back, when your money's all gone, your tail between your legs, expecting me to give you a handout. Sorry. I don't do free handouts. I don't have any more money than you. Besides, I have someone living with me..."

"You have a job..."

"What? How do you know that? You DO want something!"

"Just...I saw your name on a real-estate sign. I hoped you could help me find a place..."

"Oh, no!" Bella cut in quickly. "I'm not paying your rent, and then you cut out, again!"

"When have I ever done that, Bella? I've always been the responsible one..."

"Oh, ya. You had everything. Of course, it was easy for you to be responsible. I had little; always had to struggle. You had your marriage; a nice guy...married a rich farmer's son..."

"Not rich," Gemma objected. "We saved what we had..."

"Still had more than me...bought that pretty little cottage in that village."

"We fixed up a rundown shack; you never saw it before, we made it into our dream house!"

"And then, lost it all in the end! Was that responsible?"

"Sam...died. He got cancer."

"Right!"

Silence followed, while Bella's conscience began to prick.

Why is it we can never get along? Maybe, I am a little out of line.

Here they were fighting like two she cats, and they'd been apart for seven years.

I should be glad to see my sister...

After a long interval, Gemma quietly pleaded:

"I'm desperate, Bella...please."

"Well, you can't stay here! My boy friend just moved back in...would you like a three-some?"

"Aw...Bella...you back with that mean soldier from the states, again?"

"That's none of your business!"

Once more, a pregnant silence reigned. Guilt began riding Bella's shoulders.

"I'm sorry," she finally offered, in a strained, barely audible voice. "I never meant to abandon you...when you needed me the most. You've always been there for me...things were rocky for me, at the time. And...I couldn't bear to watch you...suffer...and die."

Damn tears! I didn't even cry at the funeral! Too darn stubborn!

"Tell you what...I'll see what I can find. What you looking for?"

"Some place away...from people. An old abandoned farm yard...maybe. Something, nobody wants. I could just stay there...till someone buys it..."

"Oh, gosh! I've got just the place. It's up north, by a lake. Too far from the road for someone to be interested. No access, you see."

"That sounds perfect..."

"Just a minute. I'll get my purse; I'll drive you up there to have a look at it..."

Chapter 17

"I owe you money," Bella revealed, contritely, as they walked the property line. "To be honest, I never thought I'd see you again, but I put it into a trust...into a savings plan, in your name. Had no idea what I was going to do with it...back when they were looking for the plane. I sold all your possessions...couldn't keep storing them. I'm sorry..."

Gem was surprised her sister was showing care at all; that she had saved her money.

"There is a considerable amount," Bella went on. "Later, people on line also gave me money...for funeral expenses. Someone put it out, that I had nothing to bury you with...I put it all in that account."

"So...you were stretching it; that you paid for a memorial?"

Bella sighed. "True. I just wanted you to go away...at first."

"You don't want that now?"

Bella avoided going there. "How about I use that money to buy the piece of property you'd like?"

Tears sprang to Gem's eyes. Such a turn around, and she hadn't even tried to mind control.

"You would do that?"

Bella nodded. "I'm ashamed of myself. I need to make restitution. I was a bitch while you were sick..."

"Oh, Bella. I forgive. You don't need to do this; especially, if you are strapped yourself..."

"That, too, was an exaggeration. My job gives commissions, plus a regular wage. I'm not hurting...really."

For a moment, she studied her shoes. When she looked up, her face showed a fondness that had rarely been there ever before.

"I need to do this. I'll even forfeit my commission. I think, with the interest the account has accumulate, plus the principal, there might even be enough to pay the full price..."

"Okay. Whatever you think can be done."

"Do you like this property? Would you want it?"

"Oh, yes. Yes!"

"That makes it easier. You see, this place is unsalable...beneath us is an abandoned mine; complete with tunnels, wrecked equipment, and fallen down shafts. Very unsafe. Dangerous. Up there in the yard, you have an opening that leads right down into it..."

Gem followed through her sister's eyes, to see off in the distance, a wooden arch, gaping darkly.

Perhaps, this place, isn't such a good idea. The boys will want to explore. They could get hurt.

"It could easily be closed off; the entrance sealed...It's not like there will be children running around..."

"And...could someone fall through...into the tunnels, I mean?"

"They tell me, those tunnels are deep, deep beneath the surface. The mine hasn't been operational for a long, long time...

"That's why I can never sell it..."

"They gave you a lemon to sell; because you are a newbie. When given lemons; make lemonade, as mother used to say."

Bella chuckled, and her sister laughed with her.

"But," Gemma observed. "I'll never be able to resell...but, then, that's okay."

"You'd sure be doing me a favor, sis...taking it off my hands."

"I think you should take the commission. Okay?"

Bella grinned. "If you say so. Now, tell you what. I'll draw up the contract. See to the lawyer; everything...and, get back to you. How do I contact you?"

"I'll meet you back at your place...when?"

"Give me...oh, say, two weeks...where do you want me to drop you off, now?"

"Just want to stay on the place...explore a while. I'll find my own way back."

Bella frowned. "You sure? It's a long way to the highway..."

"Bye, Bella. See you in two weeks."

Chapter 18

The first thing they did, when they got the legal documents, gaining possession of the land, was to set up a temporary outside camp in the trees. The keys Gem had been given were useless; the existing shack, too rundown and unlivable, to stay in; dilapidated; walls falling in; the furniture left behind, rat infected, over taken by pests, and bed bugs. All would have to be demolished.

Brad, immediately, went to crafting a large bow, complete with two dozen arrows. The wild life, in the many acres of bush, was plentiful. Surely, they could hunt on their own land. As soon as Brad was able, he did just that.

Willow went with him, operating in the same capacity she had so often on Azure Blue, as an accomplished butcher; skinner; hide preparation; and, all around cook.

As Loni and E-ri went to work demolishing the old cabin, they saved the good lumber, building with it, the smoke shack, and an underground root cellar, that could be added to later. The furnishings and rotten lumber made a great bonfire.

Gem got to work stepping out an enormous field for a garden. It was cleared, and dug, not by the men, but by Thea and Gem, using powers no human possessed. Next, it was planted, with every kind of seed they could scavenge...and yes, they pilfered those, during the night; old seeds from the back storerooms of many a nearby supermarket, where they were being stored for the next year. Growing season, according to human knowledge, was over, this far north. But, again, Gem and her blue-skinned crew, had learned methods and tricks unknown by most.

From a nursery root cellar storage, they obtained seedling fruit trees, and rejuvenated the existing neglected orchard. After all was done, they enclosed gardens and orchards under enormous greenhouse canopies, complete with blower fans for air conditioning and artificial heat. A root-seep system was installed to give nourishment and moisture.

And thus, they were equipped with a food supply.

When not helping others with their chores, Peek took up exploring. He was well equipped to work underground, so the elders were less likely to worry.

The mine shaft that led directly from the center of the yard, was his first fascination. He followed each passage right to its exit; one tunnel led all the way beneath the river; came out under a waterfall on the opposite bank.

His finest discovery came one afternoon, while everyone else was resting.

Peek found the unfinished tunnel just beneath the original homestead, not at all connected to the mine below. And here, he found gold. From then on, he spent many a sleepless night gathering nuggets, and rich dust, which he proudly presented, when the time was right.

It gave them the income to complete the compound...without robbing their neighbors.

Still, for safety reasons, they always transported their own materials, and worked under cover of darkness. They became experts at making out load bills; in the morning, the articles would be gone; the money in the till.

Also, at night, a nearby assayers office, had many a transaction they could not recall. Brad and Loni staked claim to the holdings; weighed out the ore, and easily took the money from the safe...all legal, and above board...on paper. Yet, no one ever saw them.

After many weeks, the group began to build the above ground homestead; a huge monstrosity large enough to house twelve. Always, in the back of everyone's mind, was the hope the other children would find their way home.

Loni and Brad felled the trees; Loni's laser sight, more a tool now, than a weapon. So also, Peek's wings, and E-ri's talents, made hauling the prepared logs an easier task.

In their down time, each person took up a hobby: E-ri went to building a computer/surveillance/alarm system, piece by piece, with cameras hung in the trees along the perimeter of their land. The only place he failed to place a warning beacon was in the caves...at that point, he thought, they presented no real threat, as Peek so often frequented them.

Willow went to surfing the net. It was she who found the useable furnishings people could not sell; offered instead for trade, barter, or even give away. And, the family furnished their new home in this way.

Sometimes, the boys, E-ri and Peek, went back to the city, where they had first appeared. They simply could not abandon their missing brothers and sister. Mostly...they searched for Nitha...but, after a while, discouraged, they went less and less often.

As the months passed, the boys found that city more and more degraded; a deteriorating death hole. The hospitals were in crisis. For some reason, the plague had targeted staff; doctors, orderlies, even cleaning personal, would often drop foaming at the mouth, convulsing; dead before anyone could even give them aid.

Authorities had no explanation; the victims were always male.

But Gem and Loni knew the reason. They declared, the plague, the Overseers had set loose to kill Brad, had turned on its creators.

Chapter 19

The carnival arrived at the city limits during the night; was busy setting up the rides; their trailers all parked against the outside back-ways of their self-made town. Morning was a time to feed the hungry carnivores, and stock.

Reuel watched the boy under his care; a misfit runaway who had joined the midway months ago, and been assigned to work under him. The ex-soldier could not fault the teen for the way he had joined them, for Reuel, himself had wandered in one day, confused as to who he was, having no idea, no memory of his past. That had been over five or six years ago.

But, there was something about this kid. Reuel knew he recognized him from somewhere. Though, he simply could not place him, the boy looked just like...monkey man.

Who the hell is 'monkey man'?

Reuel couldn't quite remember.

I am number one!

Now, where had that come from?

It had been a long time since he tried to remember who he was.

Faint visions of fighting, an automatic rifle in his hand; raising it to fire...into the trees.

Then a farm yard...

Monkey man! I killed it!

And then, the cloudy visions were gone.

No matter. It will come back to me...some day.

As he watched the adolescent work, feeding the large cats, his thoughts went back to that other farm yard. It was nothing like a normal farm stead: a barrier of thorn vines; gates of thin intertwined tree trunks; pigs, goats, and fowl of all kinds, both domestic and wild...

He frowned, trying to remember.

It is there; just at the edge of my mind. If I could just latch on to it. Where is that?

The thought was so elusive, yet very much real...

A place...in another dimension...another time?

Trees of bronze, rust, yellow gold...where they stood...up-side-down; like an image distorted by a camera.

What place was that? And who was I there?

That's it! I am number one!

But, who was this? Monkey man's child?

I killed that backwards creature. I cut him into pieces!

I remember it! I remember it all!

Reuel snarled deep in his throat.

It came here...to Earth! After me!

****

Storm looked up startled, at the animal growl, of the man working beside him. He shivered. and then...he recognized the cruel boss man.

For months the man had been watching him; ever since Storm had joined the circus crew; that leering, unpleasant look in his eyes, as if, somehow, he knew, Storm was not of human kind.

The boy had come through the teleport worm hole, landing in a field nearby the circus trailers; next to the animal cages. It was only logical to beg food from the workers; in return, they put him to work.

The big boss had laughed at his nakedness; said he would fit right in. At least, it had gotten him his meals, and a place to sleep.

It is no worse than I had it under Scar...

But...at the angry, malevolent glare from Reuel, Storm dropped the pail of cut fish, and...ran.

Reuel took out after him.

"You are not getting away this time, Monkey Man!" howled his nemesis.

****

Storm hid among the tents of the performers. Reuel missed where he went, ran by, searching.

The boy took off again, escaping to a nearby road. He didn't stop running, even to catch his breath, until he came to the edge of the city.

There, Storm crouched beneath a tree, gasping; winded.

****

E-ri, with Peek above in the sky for protection, was trolling the city streets again, looking for Nitha. They had lost sight of her altogether, no awareness of her essence at all, since the encounter with the street gang. Tonight, they were in a different area, one where they had not searched before, up in the industrial area; by the graveyard.

Because, the midway had come to the city, and was here on the outskirts, the boys only came in at night, if Loni and Gem were asleep. The parent couple was somewhat deficient, due to the strain on them, using their powers so constantly, in the building of the compound. The pair worried for the boys' welfare, if they knew they were away, believing more harm might arise from the carnival riff-raff.

While searching an alleyway, out of the corner of his eye, E-ri caught movement. Someone was running from one dumpster to another, hiding from him. It quickly aroused his suspicions.

E-ri turned abruptly, the memory of the last attack vivid in his mind. He made for where he'd last seen the shadow hide. Above, Peek dropped closer, hovering just above the dumpster.

A cry of fear from the shadows; then a welcome answering cry, split the silence.

Storm stepped from behind his shelter. E-ri gasped in pleasure at the Neanderthal-like twelve year old; the two boys embraced. Peek lowered gently to the asphalt, quietly chuckling.

When he stepped back, Storm was in tears; a rare condition for the stoic brown skinned boy.

"I thought I would never find you! It seems like I've been searching forever," he declared vehemently, then added fearfully. "Number One is still alive! I've seen him! And...he recognized me...he's hunting me!"

E-ri didn't exactly say it; though at that moment, he thought the bad word, that he had so often listened to, used in these streets of degradation. Instead, the expletive came out as a grunt. E-ri turned to Peek, now standing behind Storm.

"Go! Tell Loni. I'll jump Storm."

Peek nodded; took immediately to flight.

Storm nearly missed his leaving, but he turned just in time to see the black boy expand his wings, and rise in the air. The shock on his face, would have made the other boys laugh, had it not been for the gravity of the situation.

Chapter 20

Storm had always had the ability to manipulate the elements. He had shied away from controlling the weather, while he was with the midway, holding his temper carefully.

Even though they had often made fun of his ape-like features; put him in the freak show to be gawked at; considered him stupid, he had never retaliated. He had been taught hard, that virtue. He did what they wanted; acting the part; strutting about in the costume of an ape, his hairy chest exposed, face free and unmasked, hooting like the animal he was supposed to represent.

Even so, they had never truly accepted him...

Yet, the minute he and E-ri set foot in the new compound, Storm felt the unconditional love; the acceptance.

Here, no one made fun of his backward appearance; they looked past that, knew he was intelligent; accepted his unique qualities, and...talents.

Momma Gem put him right to work, causing the fog, and moisture, her plants so desperately needed.

Oh, and what gardens she had created!

Where once, he had balked at watering the fields, he now embraced the duty with excited anticipation.

His new home gave him great pleasure. Whereas, on Azure Blue, in the barnyard setting, he had been as a mere slave to Scar, his teacher; his mentor; momma Gem had always been his idol. She was the exact opposite to his master, Scar. Her love; affection; gentleness, had always been his focal point. When Storm was angry, it was Loni who disciplined him, but afterward, Gem was the one to comfort, and heal his emotional wounds.

Coming off of months in the freak show, returning to momma Gem's care was as if, as he envisioned it, he had gone to heaven.

Storm reveled in the enormous cabin; his appointed room. All to himself, yet! The freedom of walking free, without being bullied, almost stopped his small heart from beating. It did seem to have grown much larger.

And E-ri and Peek! They were more than simply brothers, now. Each male was different...just like he! Comrades; friends...together, as one.

And Peek! Wow! Those wings. They are something else!

Now, Peek was powerful! Not big. But strong!

And, Poppa Loni even treats me as a man!

Now, Storm felt more like he belonged; he was much more than a farm hand. He no longer worried about his Overseer resemblance. He was not Scar's son; never had been! No longer a blight; in his mind...nor anyone else's.

Sure, he was the result of an experiment gone wrong...just as each of the others. But, now, he had a purpose! He was treasured; he was LOVED!

Storm went to work with the other teens, willingly; no more the misfit! His duties included: protection; the greenhouses; sometimes the cattle.

A good rain was appreciated by all, even washing the cattle, and poultry.

Some nights, Storm watched the monitors with Brad, in the faint hope, he would be needed to create a whopper of a lightning storm, just to fend off some enemy.

E-ri enhanced the warning system farther. Though, there was no chance number One could have followed their escape, it was always good to be prepared.

And, finding Storm, had also renewed hope of finding Nitha. Once again, the boys took up trolling the red light district, of the city of their entry.

If Peek and Storm could find their way home, so might Lee...or Nitha.

If she couldn't come to them, THEY would find HER!

Chapter 21

Lee was dreaming. He was swimming in the sea on Azure Blue, but the lobsters were elusive. The sea was turbulent; it swelled over him, swamped him. He was beneath the waves, gasping for air, swallowing water; fighting for his life.

He cried out for momma Gem to rescue him; shouted in mind-talk, and...got an answer, but...the return was jumbled, not the sound of his momma, but the thoughts of...an infant? No, an animal.

He was on the shore, now, but the earth still rocked. The very air trembled. Bricks...rocks crumbling around him; rumbling noisily.

Momma Gem was kissing him!

But, no! That was a small, rough tongue, licking at his face. Kissing, yes...but, wet doggy kisses.

Lee opened his eyes, and remembered...

The earth about him rocked again; buildings teetered. The small spaniel whined plaintively.

Lee knew something of earthquakes. On Azure Blue there had been many such tremors, long after the explosions below ground had ceased. This was like that; his first memories of life, in the arms of his new momma. She had rescued him then, from the bowels of the Overseer caves. Dreams like this, of running with her, the minute he could toddle, hadn't plagued him in years.

Until now, he had felt safe.

But...this was different. This was actually happening; the ground was moving.

The young puppy whined again, bringing Lee to reality.

Two memory facts struck at once. First, he was on Willow's world, and second: he had appeared in a shop window in Taiwan, months ago; had survived thus far by hiding; eating scraps from the streets; stealing from produce stands, and sleeping in ditches and gullies. He was a street urchin, on his own.

Alone, he had read from the busy minds around him; learned his location, and picked up some of the sing-song, nasal language of the Asian race, who's appearance was similar to his own.

But, the terrible fact remained: he was stuck here; had no idea where his foster brothers and sisters were...those from home, back on Azure Blue, were out of his reach.

He didn't even know if momma Gem, and Poppa Loni had made it safe to this world.

Safe? Right!

This world is NOT safe...especially today.

It was rocking, again. The puppy beside him was trembling like a leaf on a windblown tree. He felt the fear in the scrawny little animal.

But...what is this? There are more...trapped?

The simple mind told him, there were more puppies, trapped under a piece of jutting concrete, in a fallen building.

Lee caught the poor animal up in his arms, and ran with him...to where he had seen, from the mind vision of the small one, the cuddle-nest, in the puppy mill.

The human tending them was dead.

Lee knelt down beside the buried, helpless creatures. The mother dog was already dead. It would not have taken long, for the puppies to starve. They were barely six weeks old; still on the mother's milk.

Lee's empathy kicked in; he knew what it was like to be motherless.

Setting down the one he carried, he attempted to lift the slab caging them in. It was easier to turn it aside. When he did, all seven wiggling balls of energy swarmed about his bare feet.

How will I get them all to safety?

Lee's eyes roved the litter about them; saw a broken wooden box upended in the street. He ran to it; brought it back, placed each wiggling puppy carefully inside, then lifted. They were heavy. But, with both arms, he was able to carry all eight dogs.

As he walked, Lee searched ahead, for a safe haven, where they might all weather the chaos about them. If this had been months earlier back on Azure Blue, he would have been too small, and too young, only five; much too weak to attempt such a feat, but as it stood now, he was on another world, older, at least twelve. He had become lithe, agile; though still skinny, he was tall and muscled, from running from irate shop owners.

****

There were still aftershocks, but Lee and his vagabond puppies had found a better spot in a park. They were nestled safely in the center opening between a group of bushes, away from the city rubble, the wreckage of buildings, and most of all...the milling displaced people. There had been a tsunami, just after the biggest quake, leaving thousands dead, or without homes. Lee was just another homeless waif.

From their vantage point, Lee and his animal crew, could scavenge undetected. Lee had taught his dogs to hunt like wild animals. They now fed themselves, and often...shared their kill with him.

Today, all were hid beneath the bushes; it was raining. They waited quietly, for the sun to come out again.

Just ahead of their hiding place, was a large square of concrete, enclosed by benches and statues. It was used as a meeting place by dissidents; anyone with a grievance came here to give voice to discontent...until law enforcement appeared on the scene.

For some unknown reason, the area was rapidly filling with people...families...children and women.

What goes on here? Why would they be meeting out here in the rain?

Something about...food relief...

The crowd began moving, as a group...

Lurking close in the shade of the trees, Lee and his pack followed after, just shadowing the group, but keeping pace, like a horde of predatory wolves.

The mob was heading into the city; trucking along at a furious pace, through the city; to the ruined airport, where they were stopped by a chain link fence with barbed wire along the top. The huge gate was barred; guard sentries held the angry, shouting beings from entering. Shouts and insults turned the air blue.

Lee remained back under the trees; told his animals to rest. He and his dogs, lay down to wait, in a nearby ditch.

Out on the tarmac, was a monster cargo plane, its belly open.

Lee was too far away to understand the words, but being a telepath, he picked out the gist; understood from the angry shouting and threats; the answers of the soldiers; that this plane held the food relief. But only certain few were to receive benefit from it.

None was allotted to these desperate people.

All through the heavy laden, storm clouded day, and into the darkness of night, Lee and his pack watched as the crates were unloaded, and hauled away. So did the women and children; some still desperately clamoring to the end.

Finally, Lee decided to find another way in. He moved along the fence, under cover of darkness, his scruffy dogs at his heels. On the other side of the compound, just as the rain stopped, and the setting sun painted the sky red in the distance, Lee found a vertical, ragged tear just along a leaning metal post.

Letting the dogs in, one at a time, Lee followed, and they trekked across the open field beyond, until they crouched at the edge of the still wet tarmac, beneath the belly of the empty plane.

The dogs were restless, anxious to pilfer from the pile of abandoned sacks on the runway, but Lee knew, there was nothing here for them...no meat.

Then, he began to reason...

If this cargo came from a place better off than here; more civilized, they will be less abusive and controlling. In another place, I could get care...and maybe, there, I might find the others...

He could easily stow away, but how to take his pack. Lee would not leave them behind.

The cargo door still stood open, a gaping, inviting hole. They were about to close it, and take off...

Lee signaled his pack animals to come round him. Then with mind pictures, and beast talk, he persuaded them inside, to hide beneath abandoned tarps, behind the empty stacked wooden platforms...anywhere that was safe.

He waited until all had obeyed. Lee just managed to hide himself, before the back of the plane slid closed.

And as he supposed, the ship took off immediately; to a better land...and he, and his mongrel band, with it.

****

But...Lee had not bargained on the base of operations being at an army training camp; in the north regions of Canada. Terrified, the boy watch as soldiers saluted; strutted with guns to their shoulders, on parade. Lee was totally unaware, this was for mere practice.

He felt certain, at any moment, these men meant to invade.

As soon as the coast was clear, Lee took his pack beyond the fence of the base camp; out into the wild wood beyond. He hoped to...safety.

But another awareness, had his heart beating swiftly; causing him soon to forget the eminent danger of the troops behind.

It wasn't long, as they travelled, that Lee picked up the familiar mind essence of a brother...

E-ri was near at hand!

But his dogs were famished. They must first, kill and...eat.

Wild animals were abundant in this woods. Here, there was no need to scavenge.

Chapter 22

They slunk into the compound like predatory wild beasts; now, sleek of coats; well muscled, from their trek across country.

When E-ri saw Lee, his vocal voice rent the silence in a jubilant shout of welcome.

Lee grinned wide, running toward his foster brother with open arms, embracing him in a firm bear hug.

But the eight full grown dogs gathered around them were unfamiliar with E-ri's scent; this farmyard was unknown to them. Until Lee silenced them, they growled viciously, low in their throats. And as they were surrounded by the other members of this humanoid clan, Lee's pet hunters had an adjustment to make; they went from protectors of the one, to part of the human pack. Here they were fed, and willingly became those that brought in the meat; defenders of all.

Lee gathered the news: everyone was present...except for momma Jewel. They told him, the Overseers had killed her.

That angered Lee!

He wanted to sig his killer pack on them right then, for killing Nitha's momma, but wisely E-ri held him back, with the promise of vengeance at a later date.

Most devastating of all...

Now, only Nitha was still missing!

Chapter 23

Nitha...

She was once called that...

But now, as the heavy, ugly, smelly male ravished her, she went to that other place...

Where she, Lee, and Peek, were flying, like miniatures of Tarzan and Jane, through bronze leaf tree tops; swinging from branch to branch, free as birds.

Bird?

Yes! In her dream-like sequence, Peek was a black bird...a predatory breed...a Raptor! He spread his wings out behind him...transparent; gossamer; ethereal. Now, he was a bat, with leather wings. He picked her up; crushed her against him...

No, no! That is this obnoxious creature atop me...this reality!

Once more, she went...other where...

Too bright! The face of an angel; holding her close.

Jewel? My momma, Jewel...

Why are you crying?

They were being mean to her. Her pain was unbearable...like fire, flooding through her body, from toes to chest; up the face, nose...to the brain.

What are they doing to you?

Gasping for air; trembling; convulsing...

Daddy...daddy! My new daddy...he's here!

Come get me, daddy...

"Oh, shit! What's wrong with this bitch?" a far away voice growled. "They gave me a sick one! This is no good! She's having some sort of fit!"

Mercifully...Nitha then found oblivion...

****

He was terrified they would accuse him of murder. He had enough of a rap sheet to put him away for the rest of his life, so he threw her body into the nearest dumpster, and took off running.

****

It was not out of neglect, nor lack of care, that they had waited this long to go out again in search of Nitha. Due to the fact that Lee and his dogs had just walked into the property, unannounced, they first spent time setting up new safe parameters, and organizing guard patrols. Then, they were ready again, to put out a full force effort to find their last missing member.

Most daylight hours, between times in the kitchen, sharing the cooking with the girls, Gem was at the monitors. Chores were done by the boys, before each went out on search duty. Noon was group nap time; the only time there was no human guard; the most unlikely time for visitors. Then the dog pack prowled...

At night, Gem again was at the monitors, as well, while either Willow or Thea roamed the property line on guard duty with Loni. Lee and Brad slept.

As for the search for Nitha, it was Brad's duty to roam the city streets in daylight. At night, Peek watched from the roof tops, while Storm and E-ri, guarding each other's backs, searched the deplorable streets.

Lee would not be left out; he and his pack went out in the wee hours of morning, returning for lunch and siesta. Sometimes, he even returned again under cover of darkness.

One morning, it was one of his dogs, who finally found Nitha...hiding, cowering, in a large dumpster filled with garbage, unable to climb out.

The pack had been given her scent and visual, through Lee's uncanny ability to communicate with them.

****

She did not know Lee. Though they had been raised together, he was now full grown; near a man. Twelve. In

120

her mind, Nitha was still, baby Nitha...helpless, unable to communicate; at the mercy of all.

She feared the large dogs...cowered away from them, and...Lee. Cringed at his touch.

Lee sat down beside the dumpster; sent his lead dog to summon Brad. The alley they were in began to brighten...

When Brad came, mercifully, Nitha knew him; she remembered...Her new daddy!

She allowed him to touch her; finally to lift her out.

But the next step was not an easy matter. It was daylight, now; nearing mid afternoon... Back at the compound, the boys would be sleeping. They were on their own.

Through streets filling with pedestrians; shops now open; police suddenly everywhere; Nitha severely beaten; obviously raped; unable to walk; they would be center of attraction; easily draw the wrong kind of attention.

The only thing was for Brad to hide with her, guarded by the two biggest dogs, while Lee stood at a short distance away, with the rest of the pack, keeping people from entering the alley.

The boy then sent his pack leader home; bearing a message: to wake Loni and E-ri, so they could jump them to safety...

Chapter 24

After months of not hearing a word from his superior, Trumack had realized, the military had never taken him seriously. Everything he had told them in confidence, was in doubt; they believed him to be unstable, hallucinating, because of the stress of losing his squad. They called it PTSD!

What a crock!

Oh, he still had all the clearances; he could call in and get any support needed, should he be on assignment, but as the psychic-counsel put it: 'he is on extended leave; opened ended.' Should he find his alien...they would look into it.

That raised Trumack's dander. Okay, he decided. He would live the life of leisure, they were enforcing upon him, and meanwhile, he would investigate on his own.

Just wish I had my number one man.

He stayed with his girlfriend, when he was in her town, way up in the boon docks: northern Saskatchewan, Canada. Most often, he trolled library records; the newspapers; internet, and the like...news broadcasts; anything that might lead him to another sighting.

His black winged boy had vanished.

But, he had traced rumors of blue skinned beings walking the streets of nearby cities at night.

And, he was not beyond rifling through his girlfriend's real estate files...

****

Trumack was looking through her papers, when Bella unexpectedly returned home, early one morning. She had forgotten a file she needed that contained her most recent sales. Among them, was the finalized sale of her sister's new property.

The man had been gone for weeks; she hadn't expected to see him again; had thought, he had disappeared once more. She had completely forgotten, he still had a key.

Trumack looked up from the sheets in his hand. As if he had not been gone at all, he assumed control, as if he owned her, and all she possessed.

"What's this?" he demanded, holding up the copy of Gemma's deed, along with her most recent bank statement. "You been holding out on me?"

From the bedroom, a second man stepped into the living area, a bowl of cereal in one hand; a spoon in the other. He appeared Arab; caramel skin tone, dark hair; soulless brown eyes...angry, vicious eyes. The exact opposite of Trumack, who had recently dyed his hair blond.

The man had obviously, also, made himself at home.

Oh, darn. Now, I have two freeloaders to deal with.

"Who is this? What is he here for? My place isn't a hotel."

"Never mind. We just found each other in the city. He's my number one man," Trumack fired back irritably. "I asked YOU a question."

Bella frowned; stepped to his side.

"Those are private," she declared, reaching to take the papers from his hands. "My work sheets."

"Not private! You've been holding out on me; you had a secret bank account." He waved the bank statement just out of her reach. "Says here, you had nearly a quarter million..."

"That wasn't mine. It belonged to my sister..."

"Your sister is dead!"

"No. Actually, just like you; she turned up one day at my door...while you were gone."

He grunted, annoyed.

"Wasn't she supposed to be on that plane that went down?"

"I guess; she wasn't. I didn't ask..."

"And, who's Brad?"

"I..." Bella faltered; peered at the sheet he held before her. "I never noticed that." The deed was made out in dual ownership. "It must be her new husband..."

"It didn't strike you as odd: she suddenly shows up, after seven years declared dead, and with a husband no less? Are you sure it was her? And not someone after the money, posing as your sister?"

"I'm sure it was her..." Bella declared in an uncertain voice. The memory of Gemma all covered up; wearing sunglasses made her hesitate.

"You stupid little fool!" Trumack exploded. "It could have been anybody. What did you do? Give her all that money , so she could buy this property? Money, I could have used for a better purpose!"

"It's not YOUR money! It wasn't even mine! It was hers! And yes, I gave it to her...to buy a place to live! It WAS my sister!"

"Right!" snarled Trumack. "I had Reuel check into where that cash came from; that money was from donations..."

"It was for her burial. I saved what was left...for her," she added lamely.

"Oh...yeah? You hid it from the government, in an account in her name. You deliberately hid it from me!"

"Okay! You want the truth? I'll tell you. Yes, I was hiding it...from vultures like you! I've learned from you; all your dishonest tricks. So, what you going to do about it? Sue me?"

"Watch your mouth, girl! I'm near at the end of my rope with you." He silently glared at her, venom in his eye.

Back by the bedroom door, Reuel chuckled at their mini war; a mere observer; enjoying the spectacle.

Bella felt she could handle her own man, but it worried her that there were now two of them. Would she be safe, if Trumack asked for help from his number one man?

I need them out of here! Need to change my locks...or go somewhere else...

"I want you to show me this place," Trumack broke into her mental scheming. "The money was yours. Okay! The property is yours!"

Before she could get out of his way, Trumack grabbed her by the hair, and headed for the door, dragging her with him. She knew not to struggle; it would only end in a beating.

"Come on, Reuel." From the bowl on the table, where Bella had tossed them, as she came in, Trumack caught up the car keys, tossing them to his sidekick. "You drive!"

****

When he saw where the place was, Trumack decided to keep his distance. They were now sitting in the car, across the river from the property, while he watched covertly through binoculars.

Among the trees he saw them: the blue skinned man and woman; even the teenage son, and daughter. They thought they were hidden, but he knew what to look for; he just hadn't expected to find them here; right in his neighborhood.

So, Bella's sister is the bitch who has been ruining every plan I've made along the line. She is the reason I can't defeat these aliens.

It made him livid.

Here I've been searching far and wide, and their hideout is right under my nose. Every last one of them, sitting here, cozy as you please.

Well, they wouldn't be for long. Now that he knew where to find them, he could put an end to them quickly.

But first, he had another matter to deal with...

The one who had helped them!

****

Trumack had moved into the back seat with Bella, while Reuel was still behind the wheel. The silence was pregnant with her boyfriend's wrath, as he watched through the field glasses.

What is he so interested in?

From here, Bella could see no one in the yard, but she noticed, there had been a lot of construction done on the property, since she had sold it: a new log house; actually...more like a mansion; dozens of huge greenhouses, and other out houses...a barn; cattle.

Where did my sister get this kind of money? I thought she had nothing.

Bella had been had but good! Her sister had conned her, just as Trumack suspected. Gemma had robbed her of her savings...Bella had made one colossal mistake.

Will Trumack take it out on me?

"Where is your sister?" His low growl made her jump.

With feigned defiance, she quickly fired back: "How should I know?"

He growled his disapproval. "You just gave her all that money. She obviously had her own stashed away. Well, I'll get this place back! Darn you! And neither you, nor she, will be around to stop me!"

Bella had no time to wonder at his meaning...

****

In one motion, the binoculars swung down, from the string around his neck, freeing his hands. He turned on her so suddenly, she only had time to back up against the seat behind her.

The blows hit hard and fast. In that small space, she had nowhere to go. It took only minutes, and her nose was bloodied.

Then, with glee, Reuel joined the fracas, reaching in between the center of the two front seats, to catch her small ears between his huge vice-like hands, and hold her fast.

Trumack's fist smashed into her face, drove the nose bone up into her cranium.

Reuel gave the head that expert twist; a crack, and the spine separated from the skull. Mercifully...

By now, Bella no longer was aware of what was going on...

She had gone to be with her Maker...

****

She wasn't very big. A little on the chunky side, but only five foot one...

Bella hadn't stood a chance...

She deserved every bit of it! Now, things are even!

Almost...

Trumack watched, standing back, his arms crossed against his chest, while Reuel dug the grave out of the hillside, and buried the body of Bella in the sand, along the river, across from her sister's holdings.

Unaware, her sister Gemma didn't even know, Bella had paid such a price for helping her.

At the time, Gem was intensely occupied in the care, and healing of Nitha's damaged mind...

Chapter 25

Thea had simply been beaten...near to death, yes, but still only beaten. Nitha had been ravished, over and over, and over, again.

It took more strength of mind, then Gem had within her, to heal this trauma. She had to enlist Thea in the healing process; show her how to help. Together, they eased and mended the broken young one, both physically and emotionally. But, ever after, there would always be scars...

This was how Thea learned compassion; empathy; and what the act of healing truly entitled: a grievous, soul and body laceration, that carried forward many years into the future.

****

"Oh, momma..." whispered Nitha in Gem's mind. "Why are human men such beasts?"

"Not every male is so," Gem comforted. "Some humans are gentle, kind; protective..." Deliberately, she projected her own memories, of a mild mannered, tender Sam; her first husband; the story book garden he had built for her."You just have to be careful whom you trust...only give yourself to one who will always put you first. He will give his life for you."

"I doubt I will ever let...another male...touch me..."

Thea cuddled Nitha close against her breast. While she and Gem, healed back from the horrendous damage they had absorbed, the young ice-skinned teen remembered her own brutal beating, and also, shivered with dread.

She had trusted...but all they did was laugh. To them, the blue sheen of her skin was not something pretty, at all; ugly; frightful; they thought her something to be mocked; teased. The huge boys had called her names...kicked her;

beat her in the face with their fists; all to bolster their ego, and hearten their waning courage.

Cowards!

"I hate them!" Thea hissed aloud. "Never will I trust a human male, again!"

"You are unbalanced," Gem soothed. "This too will pass..."

Gem hugged them both, close against her, sending good thoughts, balancing the negative emotions, so...they could go on living happy again.

But, after they were asleep, Gem also remembered her own abuse...the brutal, and vicious Galar...

Her own balance was then as precarious as that of the girls...not just against human men, but all things male...

Finally, at last, all three moved back into a semblance of balance...near whole. At least, to the view of those seeing only the outer appearance.

Chapter 26

Nitha sat sunning in the middle of the yard. All was quiet; heat steaming. She liked it like this; all alone; no one to claim her; no man to abuse.

The others in the compound were all fast asleep. It was mid-day...siesta time.

Even the dogs slumbered.

The camouflaged soldiers crept silently through the opening of the mine beneath the ground. The first Nitha knew of their presence was when a rough hand covered her mouth, to keep her from crying out. The man lifted her, struggling and terrified, trembling, so she swung above the ground.

She tried to kick him; he held her away from his chest. There was no means to send out a warning.

But, sensing the intruders, the dogs did it for her! They set up such a racket, snarling and howling, people for miles around would have heard...if there had been anyone close by.

****

E-ri jerked awake; rose up from his bed, searching with his mind.

Brad was supposed to be in the monitor room, but he had fallen asleep in the excessive heat. He started awake, his eyes immediately scanning the many screens for the intruder.

Loni was as suddenly at his side.

"Where is it? Who is it?"Brad demanded petulantly, still annoyed by the abrupt jar into wakefulness. "I must have fallen asleep," he excused."What set off the dogs?"

All perimeter cameras showed nothing but streaming heat; empty of intruders; not even a bird or wild animal.

"Where is it, Loni?"

Even Loni's psychic senses seemed dulled.

"Pan the yard camera; that's where the dogs are centered on..." Brad moved the camera above the tree swing, where Nitha loved to sit alone. "There...by the mine shaft entrance..."

"Holy!" exploded Brad. "That guy's got Nitha!"

Loni moaned audibly.

****

E-ri shook Peek. Storm sat up, immediately awake. Lee was already heading for the clamor in the yard.

E-ri quickly ordered Willow, Thea, and Gem to hide.

"No!" disagreed Thea. "I can be of help."

"Okay; then, you go get Nitha!"

Thea quickly disappeared.

****

Outside, Peek immediately took off running for the trees. To an uninformed observer, he appeared to be cowardly fleeing. But, E-ri, at least, knew otherwise. Peek was heading for the caves, to get behind the soldiers; but first, he would operate as look out in the skies above. He would tell them exactly how big was the attack.

****

Lee crept out to join his dogs. They were furiously fighting against the soldiers attempting to gain entry into the yard. The men were everywhere.

As yet, they had not had the chance to shoot their weapons; they were clubbing with the butts of their rifles, smashing at the heads of the defending canines.

Lee ordered his pack to retreat, but they were angry now. His pack snarled rejection of the mental command, unwilling to back off, but finally, they obeyed; slinking reluctantly away. Many of the soldiers were already bloodied; still they stood their ground, guns at the ready.

Lee came toward the man holding Nitha hostage, but another stepped quickly into his path.

"These your dogs?" the soldier demanded.

He stood, feet apart; machine gun at the ready, yet pointed at the ground. At ease. As if he had every right to be there.

"Yes." Lee moved to stand just in front of this leader. "What do you want?"

"This your property?"

"It's my dad's," Lee agreed, cautiously. He knew to refer them to Brad, rather than Loni or Gem, to be safe.

"Get him out here!"

Before Lee could object to the soldier's curt command, Brad stepped through the large arched entry of the monstrous cabin, from the cool darkness behind him, into the glaring sun.

"What's going on?" Brad demanded authoritatively.

"You own this property?" demanded the leader, again.

"We do."

"You got papers to prove that?"

Brad had come prepared.

Expecting such a move as this, they had purposely adjusted the title, previously, so he now co-owned with Gem; for legal functionality only, they were signed as common law husband and wife.

"Yes. Why?"

"I want to see them!"

"By who's authority?"

"National security!"

Brad realized it best to comply; held out the papers he'd had behind his back.

As the man perused them, Brad challenged him farther: "Just what is this all about?"

The man returned the papers; looked up at him, his face stoic.

"We've had reports you are harboring illegal aliens."

Brad first drew in a quick breath in shock, but quickly hid it with a disgusted laugh, immediately realizing the irony of the charge.

"And just who could have given you such information? There isn't a soul for miles around here. Nobody in their right mind..."

"So...you don't deny it?"

"No..." Brad laughed, uncomfortable. "I didn't say that!"

"Then you don't mind if we look around?"

"Yes, I do mind! Do you have a warrant?"

From the group behind the leader, a foreign soldier stepped forward. His uniform was different from the others: American military.

"I know this man! He's the one I've been looking for."

Brad recognized this man immediately; he had been leader of the charge on Azure Blue.

Did he follow us back through the portal, or what?

"His name's Brad," Trumack revealed. "I been hunting him all across the world...He's a wanted man."

"For what?" demanded Brad; shocked and indignant.

The man grinned; then hesitated. He knew there was no grounds for a charge, so he fabricated one. He had done his homework before he came.

"Child abandonment!" Trumack fired back, quickly.

"Like hell!" Brad exploded. "My daughter is right here with me!"

Brad realized immediately, to give that information, had been a mistake. He had confirmed his true identity, by just making the statement.

The lead soldier looked from Brad to Trumack, suddenly clueing in to the fact there was more going on here than he first had been told. The original purpose had simply been a way to get closer, perhaps to identify and confront.

Puzzled, the commander decided to proceed, anyway.

"How about you bring your daughter out here, so we can talk to her?" he suggested, quietly.

For a second, Brad hesitated, not wishing to expose Willow. Then, thinking it better to comply now, rather than have trouble later, he turned to Lee.

"Will you go get Willow for me, son?"

Obediently, the teen turned, and disappeared inside the cabin.

"So..." Trumack probed, smirking. "You have a son now, too?"

Brad knew he had to be quick to fabricate a believable story. If this man had done any investigation, he knew some things about his past.

"He belongs to my new wife...her kid."

"Ha!" Trumack eyed him in distain. "No record of that marriage..."

"Common law."

"How convenient! And the other girl?" he demanded, pointing to Nitha; who had succumbed to a faint of sheer fright; held limp in her captor's arms.

"My new daughter, also..." Brad agreed, scowling.

After all, it was all true; just Nitha was Lydia/Jewel's daughter, not Gem's.

Lee stepped out from the archway shadows, leading Willow by the hand.

Trumack grunted, both shocked and annoyed. He hadn't expected Brad to produce her.

"She's older than the pictures on the newsfeeds..."

Brad laughed sarcastically.

"Of course, she's older! We don't post pictures of every event, on the internet, like so many fools in this modern world...so, some perverted a-hole like you can steal our children!"

Aware tempers were flaring, the Canadian commander took over, once again.

"What's your name girl?" he quizzed, addressing Willow personally.

"Willow."

"And...is this man your daddy?"

Willow nodded, then indignantly, fired back: "Who else would he be? And he's always taken good care of me. Ever since my momma was killed!"

"And when was that?" the commander asked, calmly.

"She died...in a plane crash. It was all over the news; so anybody could read about it. I was only...little."

The commander turned to Trumack, and frowned. He was having none of this! Whatever was going on here...

"Trumack! We need a word. In private!"

As the two men stepped away to talk, Nitha began to stir. As soon as she realized there were men surrounding her, she set up a plaintive wailing, that quickly drew the attention of the commander. He turned to the soldier still holding her.

"Set her loose," he growled. "Send the kids inside!"

Willow quickly ran to her half-sister. With her arm around Nitha, she led her into the shadows of the building. Lee close behind, saw Thea, as he passed her. She stood just inside the entry, prepared to do whatever was necessary.

****

The commander returned, obviously angry; his temper barely under control.

"Sir," he reluctantly admitted to Brad. "I apologize. I didn't have all the facts when we invaded your property. We regret we have upset your family...we will leave quietly, and...not bother you again."

"Just like that?" Trumack demanded, as if he'd been the one slighted. "He's living under assumed circumstances. According to records; he's dead!"

"Looks quite alive to me," the commander returned. Ignoring the American, he turned to his own soldiers.

"That will be all, men! Let's go."

****

As the embarrassed men filed passed the mine entrance, none dared look into the shadows of the opening through which they had entered the yard. If they had, they would have noticed the dark creature hidden there. Peek sat hunched, his wings spread out...ready to pounce...and kill, if need be.

He too, had recognized Trumack...and especially, the soldier holding Nitha. Peek would always remember Number One.

Chapter 27

Through everything, Gem had always been grieving, though she had done her best not to show it outwardly. While healing Nitha's emotions, Gem's mind was often in confusion; it was not hard for the children to follow her thoughts, or find her memories.

Lately, those memories appeared intermingled into two past streams: momma Jewel's intimate friendship with Gem, and...now, scenes of Gemma growing up with Bella. And through it all, was a weaving of murder past, and either to come, or recent. Gem could not determined which, only that she was sensing...something.

And young minds listening can easily misinterpret...

That was how the young half-sisters, Willow and Nitha, discovered how their mother Jewel had died. Until now, no one had realized Gem had mind-watched the whole happening, and been helpless to interfere. Because of this, she felt extreme guilt, which surfaced during heal back.

Angrily, the sisters closed their minds, resolving to do what, at the moment, Gem could not. Hatred and vengeance, at the heartless Doctor Harmon, drove them to actions dangerous to all.

Just after the encounter with Trumack, and his number one man, the two young teens started to disappear, for long periods, off on their own. For some unknown reason, Thea joined them, enabling them with her special powers; cloaking them; jumping them...as if they were practicing for some future event.

****

Then one night Lee came home missing one of his dogs. He almost ordered; insisting Loni go out in the darkness to follow him. Loni expected to find the missing animal dead, but not...Bella's body.

Lee's lead animal sat quietly beside the buried corpse, almost as if he sensed its importance to them. The dog had never had any interaction with Bella, but it was a sensitive creature, and through contact with Lee, often picked up the knowledge of others.

He didn't howl with grief, as was often the case, were this a dead friend, merely looked mournful, and sympathetic, if that were possible in an animal.

Lee, also, had no previous connection to Bella.

But both...had knowledge of Trumack...and Number One, and the scent of the pair was everywhere.

Lee was much like an animal with his beast- sense, and telepathic beast-talk. He could smell the evil men!

****

Gem rose up on her cot, annoyed at herself. Here it was the middle of the afternoon, and she still lay mourning. Loni rested beside her. She knew it was more to comfort her, than to take a break from his labors.

Enough of this! I need to get back to reality. Bella is dead. I failed her; failed to notice when she was in trouble...wasn't there to help her...

She couldn't believe she had missed that, when it happened just across the river from the homestead.

What kind of telepath doesn't know when her sibling is dying? I should have sensed the throws of death in my sister...did I really not love her?

Her thoughts were not private. Loni heard them. He excused her.

"You were healing back," he soothed in mind-talk. "You were in emotional struggle with Nitha...her experiences; yours; and Thea's, all tangled, besides...you and your sister had been estranged for over seven years. You'd just gotten back together..."

"Still...that's no excuse. I have foreknowledge! I see...other things...I should have known!"

"Don't be so hard on yourself. You are not the Maker..."

Silently, he cuddled her close; still, she wept, and berated herself...for a sister unknown; time lost, never to be retrieved...

It is all so...pointless. This mourning the lost, or what might have been...

"Enough of this!" Gem finally declared aloud.

Beside her, Loni opened his eyes; he had fallen asleep.

****

That morning, they had given Bella a proper burial, out in the field beyond the greenhouses. All around, in a rectangle, they had planted tiny seedlings, leaving spaces for other family members; somehow, they knew, this would not be the last of the causalities.

It's just too bad, we have no body for Jewel...maybe, a memorial plaque...

****

Loni knew she needed to vent. He would not let her up; kept her from scurrying away to make the next meal.

"Talk to me," he suggested, in mind-talk. "Show me your worries. Let me help...with the pain."

She sighed. He knew her well by now.

"It is not simply the grief, Loni," Gem admitted. "There is much more to it."

He nodded. "Tell me..." he encouraged.

And so, propped back against his chest, Gem began to bear her soul.

"I am worried for the young ones; for the girls...so battered; and...E-ri. He is so...angry."

He closed his eyes sensing her agony, but agreeing, just the same.

"My world has become such a violent society," she went on. "We did not prepare our children for constant conflict between the races; the prejudices of color; and between male and female. They are still so young. What if something happens, and we are no longer here to guide them? To teach them..."

"We taught them to trust the Maker. We have done our best to show them a better way."

"But, right now; it seems all our efforts have gone by the wayside. Both E-ri and Thea have already been attacked for the very color of their skin. Because of fear! Judgment should not be made due to appearance; it should be governed by behavior. If a man...or woman, chooses to be evil: greedy; violent; a pervert; a rapist; to see the opposite sex as property to be exploited; or only to be used for pleasure...then yes! Punish her...or him, according to his crime.

"I am not against that! These things are what should be judged unacceptable! But the sentence should not come about because of where you were born, or the color of your skin; not your size or age; neither to what god you pray...or what can be done with your mind.

"Attitude! What is in the heart! Your inner balance of good and evil: kindness, love...charity. The tongue and actions...that is what is important..."

Loni knew she was only finding the way; she needed to get it all out. He remained quiet; listening at her back.

"I fear for E-ri. He would like nothing better than to kill every Overseer spawn; castrate each human male; wipe this world of all its inhabitants, and Loni...I can barely blame him, considering what has been done to his sisters. He sees no good in the race I came from..."

"Nor, at the moment, do I," the ice-skinned male agreed, coldly. "But...then, I know better than to judge. I came from a race judged, tortured, put down for being...different."

"I grieve for this world," Gem added in compassion. "There are good beings here, but so few, it seems, they can make little difference. The evil is winning. All the striving and struggle, and...our children must grow up here? We HAVE nowhere else to go..."

Silently, Loni pondered the dilemma. Gem continued her soliloquy:

"I look around at the nature I grew up with...It has always been my comfort; a positive. Back on Azure Blue the trees housed us. I loved flowers, and waterfalls; just to look at! But some were for food, also. The animals fed us, clothed us; helped us...as long as we kept them well fed and safe. They gave us what was needed, even though we had to struggle hard to get it. And, I know...the Almighty Creator made it all...for OUR benefit; made that environment good...for us! Blessed us...both there, and...here!"

He decided to play devil's advocate.

"Yet," he declared. "In this world, your people have taken it all for granted; they abuse resources, refuse to share...worship the created, and not the Maker. How is that fair?"

Tears sprang to her eyes. "I know!" she cried. "And that's what grieves me the most. Since I left, my people have turned away from believing. And nature shows it, too! No more can I feel that closeness to my Maker! It is like He has abandoned this world to the Overseers!"

Loni could not help but agree. "Sometimes," he added. "It looks to me, like the human race, the supposed intelligent species here...is the parasite. The young start out perfect, then somehow are infected just by being born...or coming here!"

Gem shivered. "Oh, no, Loni," she objected, softly. "The element lacking here is...love. Forgiveness...no judgment..."

"Ah...yes." He smiled, triumphant; he had turned her mind back to the right. "When we learn to forgive; overlook...forget and go on. Don't hold the past against the doer...

"If E-ri, or any other, chooses to retaliate, to go to the violent side, we cannot stop him, or be held accountable. The Almighty governs behind the scenes. He gave us all free will. It will be on their consciences, how they live. They must learn the hard way. We can only guide...

"We are not pawns here. Remember, nothing happens without a purpose; some things are for teaching; others for discipline...to guide and direct us forward." He gulped in a labored breath, remembering his own childhood. "Hard!" he admitted.

Sadly, Gem agreed. "It is not just Overseers; the leaders...or the criminals. The evil is in all of us: male, female; teen...even the infant. The enemy is within us! And outside, too...plaguing us. The demon; Evil!"

"We let it in...nurture it..." he countered, quietly. "Only the Maker can expel it..."

"But...since we came here...we cannot seem to let Him...we fight Him off...instead of repelling...the evil," Gem returned regretfully. "Our nature...fights to conquer, control...for possession. We always want our own way..." She sighed. "And that is what the young ones are up against...not these minor surface problems..."

"Seek the Maker," Loni declared quietly. "We are all guilty; each of something offensive: anger; revenge...seek His forgiveness; learn and go on. Ask the Creator to cleanse us of the inclination toward evil...we can only...try."

"I fear... Will the children learn this? Without Elders to guide them? In time..."

"Did we?"

Chapter 28

"Where are the girls?" Gem sat forward abruptly, searching with her mind. The kitchen was unusually silent for that time of day.

By now, the boys were up, and out doing chores. They could find Brad's thoughts in the monitor room. But, female presence, from the kitchen, was absolutely nil.

Loni quickly scanned the compound with his seeker sense. Now, the boys and Brad also, were aware of the frenzied mind-search for the three girls; all were always telepathically intertwined with their leaders.

Brad quickly searched each screen. It was all muggy hot again; no sign of the young females. Harvest was the beginning in the district; the busiest and hottest time of the year.

Playing games again; hiding...why?

Gem rose quickly, heading to the kitchen to begin the supper meal.

There is no use getting upset; we have work to do.

"I'll check the tunnels," Peek offered, and was off.

Gem yelled after him, in mind-talk. "Don't fly out in the open. It's still too light out. You'll be seen! The soldiers could come back, and we can't afford to lose even one of you."

"Why would they take off like that?" mentally demanded Brad in annoyance.

Gem and Loni had already reasoned it out. E-ri grunted, as he read their unguarded communication.

"What?" Brad enquired in mind-talk. "I'm their father. Don't keep me in the dark. I wasn't born telepathic. You taught me to read, but I'll always be slow at it. I didn't follow all that, so...Just tell me!"

"Nitha...and Willow, too," Loni offered, hesitantly. "Nitha wants revenge..."

"Against? Who? For...what was done her? Where'd they go?"

"To the hospital," Gem offered. "They want to avenge their mother's death. They seek Jewel's killer..."

"Doctor Harmon!"

Gem gave a mental nod.

Storm, listening in, threw in a question: "And...Thea?"

"She went along...to protect them. She always does," Gem admitted. "She jumped them from by the waterfall entrance in the caves."

"Those stupid kids!" Brad exploded aloud, to the empty room in which he sat. "That Nitha's not quite all there since she returned! But, why wouldn't Willow have the sense? I thought she was smarter than that! Kids just don't think...the consequences...Man!"

Ignoring Brad's rant, and his insult to their junior intelligence, Lee broke in. "What can we do, momma?"

"Nothing. For the moment...after dark...we will all head out, and search for them."

"By then...they could be in the hands of the...Overseers," Brad moaned hopelessly.

"It will serve no purpose, if we, too, are taken. Everyone, do your jobs, and...stay put!"

Gem sent a command to Peek, as well: "Peek, just watch at the waterfall, for their return."

"Maybe, they'll see the futility of the idea, and just come back," Brad reasoned, hopefully.

****

After the evening meal, Brad and Loni kept watch on the monitors, while the boys helped Gem gather ripened produce from the gardens. Because of this heightened observance, the two males were not caught off guard a second time, as a new dual invasion began, by the mercenary soldiers Trumack had gathered together.

"Holy!" exclaimed Brad, pointing to the monitor of the entrance shaft across the river. "Look there! Oh, Blast! It's that darn soldier again...sneaking in a second time. What is it with that man? Can't he let it go?"

"You do realize who that is?" Loni challenged, quietly.

"I know!" Brad exploded, angrily. "He's the leader of the special forces men that plagued us back on Azure Blue."

"And...Bella's killer," Gem added from behind them, as she entered the kitchen with a full basket of corn to shuck.

"And..." offered E-ri, following her in. "The other...is the one who shot Peek."

Standing behind, in the entrance way, Storm gave a shiver of dread, as he envisioned a premonition, anticipating the future. He put down his load of harvested tomatoes, and vegetables.

"I can't do much in those tunnels," he complained.

"Nor, I," Lee agreed, his arms loaded down by a canvas bag of ripe fruit. "The dogs will get hurt. One could go over a cliff..."

"We should have blocked off that entrance, instead of just putting up cameras," Brad reprimanded.

"Too late," Loni stated. "We'll work with what we got. You boys stay here; just E-ri, come with me."

"No!" Gem quickly objected. "E-ri stays behind. Tonight, he and Peek can go into the city and find the girls. I'll come with you, and deal with these intruders."

Loni knew better than to argue with his mate, but as they left, he fired a final order, back behind him.

"Brad; you're in charge. Boys! Guard the compound!"

Chapter 29

Reuel led the way. He always took front point. After all, he was Number One. Always would be; to his dying breath.

They had already passed under the river bed, through the dripping corridor, a dark tunnel, interwoven with large tree roots, that appeared about to collapse.

Overhead, a dark shadow fluttered across the wall beside him. Reuel raised his eyes to the cavernous space above. He couldn't see up very far; the roof was too far above, beyond his vision range, but he thought he saw a black winged shape.

Probably, just a bat. The distance distorts the shape.

Intent on gazing above, distracted, he almost stepped off the ledge. Trumack jerked him back, just in time.

"Damn! That was close!" Still shaking, he moved back; turned into a side tunnel that was safer.

"You sure this is the way we went last time?" Trumack demanded, annoyed. "Or, are you about to get us lost again?"

"I know my way in!" declared Reuel, indignantly.

****

Lee had taken his dogs out to guard the perimeter, beyond the last greenhouse. At the moment, he knelt on one knee, holding his lead dog by the scruff of his neck, his arm across the back of the animal.

The dog had just gone tense; she had picked up a scent.

"Easy girl. What do you smell?"

Evil. Evil human. Soldier men.

"Where?" challenged Lee.

Coming through by the graves. Many!

Lee nodded silently. He could see them now, too.

As he released his lead lady canine, he gave orders, in beast-talk, to the minds of all his pack.

"Get them!" he snarled aloud, just below the range of the human ear.

And then, the invaders suddenly found themselves in the fight of their lives.

****

Somehow, one soldier got past the vicious, occupied dogs, by moving alongside the outermost greenhouse. He took refuge inside; a mistake he would live to regret.

Inside, he felt reasonably safe. The plastic wall sheeting rattled in the wind; the interior was growing dim with the dusk from outside.

He looked about at the raised beds of vegetables, and then...it began to rain.

Inside? Since when does it rain inside a building? Must be some sort of sprinkler system. But why, is it needed...when they have a drip watering system to feed among the roots?

Puzzled, the soldier looked to the roof.

He had been raised on a market garden estate; he knew, seldom did they use both systems together. In the rafters, he found no evidence of piping or sprinklers.

What he did find, terrified him.

Thunder clouds, low and forbidding; as if this was outside, in the open air. And lightning, shooting from cloud to cloud, like luminous streaks of power, thrown from the god of thunder's hand.

A terrible storm was brewing. Inside! Where it should never be.

He shivered; turned to run.

The door slammed shut.

****

Storm was angry; very angry. Livid, in fact.

This animal dares to hunt us! Like we have done something wrong...just because we were born different. I've just had enough of this! If the monsters can water-board us, why can't we do the same to them?

Storm remembered, how Loni had described the method used to torture Scar, to gain his submission...even before, the backward male was finally beheaded.

Soldiers are scum; the lowest of creatures...even beneath me!

The dying vision from the past, that Gem had intercepted, of Scar's last moments, fled through the teen's thoughts. He had not meant to intrude, to see such a thing, but he had read it, by accident, in one of her unguarded moments.

Storm was the one who most resembled the half-male Neanderthal, Scar, from back on Azure Blue. Though in real life, the boy had not ever wished to be known as like him, now, Storm considered Scar father-like; the closest likeness to himself.

Storm growled, imitating Loni, as he was want to do, when he was frustrated. Yes! Storm was more than frustrated!

The unfortunate soldier had taken refuge in the cubbyhole for storage; to escape the deluge Storm had conjured up. The teen ran forward, slammed the door on the small room, leaning against it, so the intruder could not push it open. The man was now trapped!

Storm moved a cloud within the confined windowless shack, and the plywood room began filling with water.

Soon, Storm could hear the man struggling to keep his head above the water line; the gurgle, as he gasp water into his lungs...

But, somehow, it did not give him the pleasure he sought.

A new thought plagued him.

Scar wasn't killed by the water-boarding...

How many times had Loni warned him about this anger of his; told him, he needed to let it go, so he would not harm another?

I am killing...Loni says, we should never kill. It is the Creator's place to avenge. What am I doing?

But...in the end, didn't the Number One soldier behead Scar? They had also beaten Loni; nearly killed HIM!

Yet, Loni's words came back to him, filling his mind. The full force of guilt pounded at him.

"If we kill, we are no better than Overseers! The Maker didn't create you for evil. You were made, given your power, to do good!

Storm felt like weeping.

I am evil! I am killing!

"No matter what is done to you," Loni's voice came back in memory. "It is never an excuse to kill!"

Inside the shed, the rain finally stopped. Immediately, the water began to recede, to seep away into the bare ground beneath. The prone soldier was revealed.

Oh, it's too late. Too late...

Storm tore open the door; rushed forward to the side of the unconscious man. He wasn't much older than Storm...

The man was no longer breathing.

Storm bent over him; covered his mouth with his own, as he had seen others do, to revive a drowning victim. He blew in. Then, pounded the chest. Why, he hadn't a clue. Repeated the procedure.

Suddenly, the young soldier coughed, gagged. Storm stepped back, as he rolled over, and vomited water.

Storm, then, crawled away; hid, so he wouldn't be seen; ashamed of his actions.

The young soldier sat there, dazed. Suddenly, after many minutes, he shot to his feet as if in panic, scanned the darkness around him, and perhaps decided, there was no one else around. He seemed confused; as if he felt everything that had happened was a figment of his imagination.

Finally, after a time, he made for the door. Again, he hesitated; as if he was reluctant, or didn't remember, he should return to the hunt for the residents of the property. At last, he took off, but not toward his comrades. No, he turned toward the field beyond, and hightailed it away as fast as he could.

At least, I discouraged one...

Storm shivered. How close he had come!

Chapter 30

Thea came visible in a hospital stairwell, holding hands with her two friends, one on either side of her. Willow, the newest addition to the lifelong friendship between Nitha and Thea, was trembling, not with anticipation, but fear dread, as she let go.

"Where is the Doctor?" wondered Nitha in mind-talk.

"In the next room; his office...eating lunch," Thea supplied. "He's alone..."

"Okay. You two stay here," Nitha ordered.

Nitha always used mind-speak, because she stuttered so badly, and Willow had learned to follow along; reading her sister easily, and projecting her own thoughts in return, despite being Earth born. Now, she objected, in that manner, with force.

"No!" Willow insisted. "I'm coming with you! I want to confront that murdering monster, too. Jewel/Lydia was my mother, also."

"Oh. You don't think I'm going to wait in here by myself," objected Thea indignantly. "I'm not leaving you two on your own..."

Nitha shrugged. Willow answered for her:

"If anyone sees you..."

"Let's go. I'll stay invisible."

The other two were agreeable with that.

****

Harmon was still disconcerted; the whole story seemed incredible. It had shattered his secure, imagined safe haven; upended his composure.

One of his lesser physicians had brought forth the story; a psychiatrist serving in another facility. He had seen an outpatient to fill out forms to prove the man still incapable of duty; not even a Canadian; an American soldier suffering from PTSD.

It was when the physician read the man's history, that the Overseer world was rocked. The soldier told of entering another world through a portal from the sea, out in the Bermuda triangle, while investigating the wreckage of a downed plane; later sent with a task force; finding blue-skinned individuals on the other side; battling unbelievable psychic powers, and at last, following them through a second portal to this world. Under cover of his illness, he was still tracking a blue-skinned man, or woman, he believed was somewhere in this world.

The man, himself, had gone missing for seven years...

To make matters worse, the patient appeared totally unaware, he had been talking with an Overseer from that very alien world he spoke of.

A little knowledge was most dangerous, especially if he continued to investigate. Also, with his superiors involved, even if they did not believe...

This was the only thing that saved the man's life. At another time, the Overseers would have taken quick action. Instead, unbeknownst to the patient, the psychiatrist simply fitted him with a tag, to keep track of him.

The whole matter had totally rattled Harmon. To realize the military of this world knew about them; not to mention the blue-skinned race...that there was one of that species still alive...AND on THIS side of the portals...

What do I do about it? The stupid human hunts right on our doorstep!

Preoccupied, Harmon sat absorbed in his thoughts, his sandwich forgotten; the magazine he was supposed to be reading up-side-down without his being aware of it.

****

Doctor Harmon continued to pretend to be reading his medical journal; eating a sandwich. The door slid open a crack, then, opened wider.

He grunted, annoyed, but did not look up, his mind distant; literally, in another world.

"I'm on a break," he growled, petulantly. "It can wait!"

****

Willow held the door wide, just long enough to make certain Thea, too, had stepped inside. After Nitha, she, herself, entered.

Carefully, Willow closed the door behind them.

She waited a second, just to make certain the man went back to what he was doing. It appeared, he thought they had withdrawn, when the door closed.

The man didn't look any different than the average human. If he had sported the headgear, and flowing robes, he would have resembled an Egyptian Arab. A huge man; dark hair; brown eyes; large nose; heavy solid build; at least more than six and a half feet in height, when standing.

Willow noticed, the magazine he held was up-side-down.

He's not really reading. What's that about?

To look at him, you would never know he was an Overseer...or from another planet. But, the girls knew otherwise.

Nitha had expressed the wish that Willow be the spokesperson. The Earth born girl gathered the words in her mind.

"YOU..." she hissed aloud. "Killed my mother!" Accusation and hatred warred thick in her voice.

His head shot up in shock.

"YOU made an orphan of Nitha!"

He drew in a sharp breath; appeared to regain his equilibrium; fired back, indignant.

"I have no idea what you are talking about! Who are you, anyway? Who let you in here?"

His large left hand was feeling for something beneath the desk.

A button! He's calling security!

Her thought was enough to warn Thea. The invisible blue-skinned girl moved directly behind him.

Just before Harmon could press the device, he seemed to freeze, as if paralyzed, his hand on the button, unable to press.

Willow snarled, like one of Lee's dogs; her wrath suddenly boiling over.

"You had no compassion; no feeling at all for her situation. You just took her life, as if it meant nothing. A needle in the arm..."

Comprehension flooded his features.

"I'll teach you a lesson! You won't get away with this! You don't mess with us!"

His eyes showed he had connected the dots. Frozen in motion, he tried to speak. His lips moved, but all that came out was a soft, whispered gibberish...

She read denial in his mind; glowered at him.

He began to shake.

"Not so brave, now. Are you?"

Finally, he got a quiet word out.

"What are you...going to do...to me?"

"I SHOULD kill you...like you did my mother...or make you a blithering idiot. To begin with...how would you like to be an icicle?"

Thea's voice from the empty air behind him, made him start.

"Don't kill, Willow...you are better than that."

Willow thought on that a moment.

No. I'm not a killer...not one of these heartless beasts...

"He deserves it!" she declared aloud. "The way he tortured, with his drugs. To him, she wasn't even a person..."

"Won't bring her back," Thea argued, from behind the man. "If you kill him, it makes you just like him."

Beside Willow, Nitha growled her disapproval. Thought projecting loud enough so the physician heard as well, she ordered the opposite of what Thea was suggesting:

"Make him feel all that's done to him, Thea!" Her audible thoughts echoing in their heads, Nitha pleaded with the invisible being. "Heighten his senses! So he feels it intently..."

"Will that make you both feel better?" Thea demanded.

That brought the other two near to tears. Both shook their heads, realizing the blue-skinned girl was correct.

But, Willow was resolute. "Thea? Protect Nitha, while I do this...please."

"I will...if you do not kill."

Willow nodded agreement. To the man, she ordered: "Stand up! Come here!"

He found his paralysis lessened, and obeyed, hesitantly. He moved out from behind the desk, as if he were a puppet on strings.

Willow closed her eyes; let fear overwhelm her.

A deadly chill filled the room. Doctor Harmon began to shiver; frost formed on his face; panic filled his features. He tried to move, but again, was, somehow, prevented. Ice spread down his chest; up into his hair...down his arms; then the legs. He stood...like a frozen statue, an ice sculpture of a man. Only, the dark brown eyes, in contrast, against the stark white of frosted features, moved fearfully; groping about, seeking for mercy, fearfully, hopelessly.

"I could have killed you," Willow informed him coldly. "If I'd touched you; if I even did it now...you'd crumble into a million pieces. That's more chance than you gave my mom..."

His eyes actually filled with tears.

The others in the room waited with bated breath. Finally, Willow spoke again.

"Okay, Nitha." Her voice held an ominous threat of deeds to come. "Now it's your turn!"

The eyes of the man filled with terror. Willow got the impression he was praying...to whatever god he believed in...if he had any faith, at all.

Thea came visible, expertly reading his thoughts. "He wants to know, what you are going to do with him..."

Willow grinned. The man was at their mercy, just as their mother had been in his hands.

"Let's see," Nitha projected. "I could send him someplace VERY HOT!"

Willow laughed. "Maybe...the sun?"

"No." objected Thea, quietly. "That would kill, and...he wouldn't remember...what we can do."

Nitha nodded. "Where?" she asked of her older sister.

Suddenly, Willow chuckled out right, amused at her own deviousness.

"I have the perfect place!" she declared. "Lock him in a drawer in this hospital's morgue freezer. There, he will thaw out gradual; scream and yell for help, 'till someone finally finds him...learn what it feels like to be...among the dead."

From the power of Nitha's mind, a small portal opened just in front of the man. She moved back, so as not to be sucked in with him. The mighty Overseer Doctor was sucked away, vanishing from view. Nitha did not even have to speak the destination; each knew where the man could be found.

As the portal closed, and evaporated, Thea quickly stepped forward, and grabbed her two foster sisters by the hand.

"Someone's at the door," she revealed in mind-talk, as all faded from view. They had almost been caught off guard.

The door opened; a nurse's head poked in.

"Doctor Harmon?" She stepped in, looked around; found the space empty of visible persons. "I thought, he was in here? Burr...it sure is cold in here."

Turning about, she left the room, shutting the door behind her.

The three girls came visible again.

"That was close!" Thea exclaimed.

Willow's conscience was beginning to prickle. Tormenting the guilty had not been as rewarding as she had hoped; had not eased the grief. Instead, it was replaced by a deep foreboding...a need for correction...or perhaps, even...punishment.

Willow, the oldest, had taken the lead, but it had been Thea, of a different species, who had been the voice of reason. And Nitha, Willow's baby sister, though angered as much as she, had merely gone along with the crowd.

Some example! She, Willow, was the instigator, the rebellious teen. She had led the others to do this heinous act. She was the most guilty!

Never before, in her young lifetime, had she so rebelled. She had always been a follower; her father's obedient daughter. What had come over her? How had she stepped so far away from her upbringing?

Willow shivered.

"Let's go home," she suggested, her voice filled with regret.

Chapter 31

Gem could feel the pulse as soon as she encountered the two soldiers; that deadly, debilitating, high pitched hum, that had the power to weaken her to such a point, as to render her ability neutral. Only once previously had she been affected by such a powerful ray, and that time it had come about by accident, in the slaughter barns on Azure Blue; the living space of Galar, when he had held her prisoner.

She had known there were two types of devices used by the Overseers, to control their subjects; Gem simply hadn't realized, the second was used here on her home world. She wasn't expecting it.

The first was a simple tracker the Overseers implanted in most of their grown experiments, slaves, and kidnapped, other world, breeder females. They were meant to merely help find escaped or missing subjects.

She and Loni had safely removed their trackers from themselves, and the children.

The second form of implant was the one that could do the blue-skinned race harm; this one, was the one Gem was unprepared for here. It contained a dampener, an infinitesimally tiny, clear crystal that melded into the skull, totally undetectable by x-ray, or any other imagining machine. It actually blocked the viewer from seeing anything, scrambling the screen like a faulty, snowy television channel. The device was only visible to the original, alien, parent, machine.

This type of tracker left a human in control of his own faculties, until the Overseer desired otherwise, but then, he could be controlled, or subjugated, even annihilated as the master so wished.

Trouble was, such a device, back on the home world, had mostly been developed for just one purpose: to control and eliminate the blue-skinned race. Because of this species' psychic abilities, the tracker was meant to diminish their powers, with a soundless pulse, only they could telepathically hear. If increased in intensity, it would kill, or reduce the subject to mere infantile reasoning, and obedient subservience.

It was seldom used for the lower type humans of Earth, but even these, especially the males, could be controlled by such a device, and made to do unspeakably horrendous acts to others or themselves, simply by bypassing the subject's own will.

From the moment that Gem encountered Trumack, the pulse was devastating. His tracking device had been implanted just behind his right ear, and was emitting a powerful incapacitating whine only she could hear. It made her near sick.

Oh, mercy! The Overseers have found him! Are tracking him...right into our carefully established safe refuge...

The pulse had an extensive range. Gem couldn't even give warning. Any Blue-skin, even a genetically altered human, entering the tunnels, would be rendered helpless, powers, useless; no more efficient then a normal human being.

To top it off, because Gem was originally blind, it now rendered her totally sightless.

How will we fight this evil man?

Loni suddenly came up on the perimeter of the field...and immediately felt the effects, as well. He gasped in shock; realized a sudden loss of hearing; became disoriented.

And because, she used him as her eyes, that made Gem not only blind, but deaf, as well.

****

Reuel came face to face with the ice-blue woman first; almost collided with her. It was as if she were blind, and couldn't see him until she touched him. Once she knew where he was, she locked onto him in a tight body clench, and held on.

Behind him, a male blue skin came up on Trumack, and for the first time the two men noticed the alien's eyes. Although they were turquoise, the center slit was vertical, like those of a feline.

They should have been able to see in that darkness, for both their skin, and their eyes were luminous, yet the pair moved as if deaf, as well as blinded.

"Watch out," warned Trumack, landing two blows, rapid fire to the body of the male. "They have powers."

"What sort of powers?" gasped Reuel, as he struggled with the female. She certainly wasn't using anything but her hands.

"The kind that can send you away...to another place..."

Suddenly. Reuel remembered: the explosion of bright light, just before he had left that alien world; and the angry little girl that had been standing over him, yelling: 'You hurt my daddy!'

He shook his head to clear it, and his free left hand went to his boot for his knife.

"But...this one looks different then the little girl," he objected.

"Doesn't matter," Trumack returned. The smaller blue-skinned male danced a desperate dance with the camouflaged soldier, fists flying. "These are the parents," Trumack grunted. "I think, they've been hiding down here."

"Then...why don't they use those powers on us?"

"Maybe, they are non-violent? Who knows?"

The woman just wouldn't let up, and the blue man was stronger than he looked. He was getting the upper hand on his boss.

Something has to be done to turn the tables!

"Club him!" shouted Reuel.

The woman kept pushing him back the way they had come, so he couldn't offer help.

"Can't," Trumack grunted. "Dropped my gun when we first connected."

And Reuel realized; so had he. He had done it deliberately, thinking it useless here, in the narrow tunnel, and a woman an easy mark to overcome. Oh, he had been so wrong!

Just then, he finally got his knife free. He came up with the wicked blade, in a slice that would have easily cut any man's throat. But just at that moment, she ducked.

He missed her throat by inches, sliced at her face. She didn't see it coming.

****

It was shock, more than anything, that made Gem cry out. She shouldn't have been vulnerable; the blade should not have even punctured the skin; yet the sharp blade cut deep, and to the bone. The wet blood began oozing down her cheek immediately; disorienting pain froze the side of her face. She tasted the copper tang of her own life blood.

Without thinking, her hand went to her face, and she stepped back. Only to find, she was teetering on the edge of one of the many precipices from which she could fall to her death.

It had been discovered, the caves beneath the property were not simple caves, but multi-facetted tunnels of an abandoned mine, complete with discarded track, and open rail cars to haul the ore. Most of the many storied facility was fallen down; girders given way, some half broken, some upright struts waiting to impale you. This had been the real reason no one would purchase the property.

Worst of all, were the ledges, at many levels, from which, if you were not careful, one could so easily fall to your death. It was such a shelf on which she presently tottered; swaying dangerously.

As Gem turned aside, the man she struggled with rammed her hard against the back wall. It was then, he too, realized how close to the edge they were. He rocked, unbalanced, on the edge, dropped to his knees for safety, and still holding the knife, came at her again.

But, Gem was more concerned with warning her mate.

"Loni! Look out!" she warned telepathically. "We are at a drop over into the lower caverns."

"I suspected as much," he returned in mind-talk. "I can hear the rushing water...through their ears. We are near the falls."

****

Peek could hear them fighting; the men yelling to each other. He took to wings, heading into the tunnels, to bring rescue. But as he drew near, he became exceedingly disoriented.

Even though the expansive interior of the caverns had never hindered him before, he was now having difficulty flying. That had not happened since he had first learned to fly; the first time he had gone airborne.

There was a constant hum in the air...

Or is that in my mind?

Peek kept hitting the walls, like a bat that had lost its echo location.

What is that god awful sound?

As he got closer to the fighting, it got worse; the closer he came, the more trouble he had navigating.

How am I going to be of any help?

He came upon them struggling; two pairs on the brink that dropped into the unknown: Momma Gem and the smaller soldier; a knife clutched in his fist. Poppa Loni matching fisticuffs with the bigger one called Trumack.

Why don't they use their mind powers? Too dark down here?

That blasted hum!

It was coming from the bigger soldier...

The man struggling with Momma Gem was pushing her toward the edge... Loni was trading fist blows with Trumack...

It all happened too quickly for Peek to think clearly. He simply reacted.

One last push, and Gem went over the edge backwards.

Loni broke free, but just before poppa made it to the edge, Trumack, close on his heels, rammed his head back against the rock, hard enough to confuse him. Still, in the seconds following, not thinking clearly, attempting rescue, Loni made it to the rim, and jumped after his mate.

From where Peek hovered at a distance, he saw when Loni lost consciousness. The reaction of the blow delayed, his body seemed to sag suddenly, and simply go limp.

With terror, Peek realized, both foster parents could not help themselves. And...he could only save one at a time. Even with his powerful wings, he could only carry one heavy adult in an upward swoop.

Peek dove down past the ledge, his legs hanging forgotten, not drawn up as usual. One leg connected with the shoulder of a laughing Reuel, but Peek never noticed. That incessant hum was driving him to madness. He couldn't judge his distance; he went where he did not plan...his flight erratic.

The impact of Peek's foot, sent Reuel over the edge with the two blue-skinned warriors. Now, not two, but three were falling...

Oblivious, Peek dove.

Which parent do I save? If I can only clear my head...
As he flew deeper, the hum seemed to lessen...
But, will my head clear on time?

****

Trumack saw the black shadow. It passed over head so rapidly, he had no time to identify what it was. Besides, he was more interested in what was going on below.

163

He dropped to the edge to watch; gasped in shock, and disbelief, at what he saw.

A bat-like man?

That's when something hit Trumack hard from behind. He had not seen it coming; never realized there were other aggressors in the tunnels.

He barely had time to keep his balance; he dug in his boot toes, hard.

Chapter 32

E-ri was finished with his chores; the other boys were handling the invaders easily: Lee with his dogs, on attack mode, and Storm had created an early evening thunder shower, that made it difficult for the troops to penetrate further into the yard...and as for Peek; E-ri knew he had gone to the waterfall entrance to be of help inside the tunnels. The girls had still not returned...

But he felt, searching for them could wait. It was more important to get rid of the intruders.

E-ri felt he wasn't needed out here, so...he went to join Brad at the monitors.

"Can't see a thing!" Brad grumbled when E-ri entered. "Something is scrambling the camera output in the tunnels. Something's not right...I haven't gotten any mental read from either Loni or Gem, either. How about you?"

E-ri had been too busy following what was going on in the yard; he had thought his foster parents simply too occupied to send out any mind-talk. But, now he thought about it, it was unusual, he saw no visual in his head.

He shook his head in answer to Brad's inquiry. He touched the delinquent screen, trying to bypass whatever caused the disturbance, but nothing made a difference.

"I can't fix it," he admitted, stepping back. "I'm going down to help..."

As E-ri turned to leave, Brad shot a warning after him: "Be careful. I have a bad feeling about this."

It was rare, Brad was the one to take note of intuition. Forewarned, E-ri slipped into the darkness with caution; chose to walk in rather than teleport.

Still, he ran...at a speed no eyes could follow...until, he encountered the mind-confusing, vibrating hum.

****

By the time E-ri reached the battle, it was all over. He was too late to actually be of help. His parents were already over the edge; Peek diving for them, and the man, Trumack, was kneeling at the edge looking down.

Anger boiled within E-ri, but the incessant drone of sound in his head confused his thinking. He did manage to surmise, the noise made him powerless. It was why his parents had been conquered; injured or...worse.

If I have no abilities, I have to use human methods...

He had no time to assess the situation below. E-ri went for the kneeling man, whose attention was elsewhere; vulnerable.

The teen, in his mind, meant to kill, as he rammed the soldier from behind, but he hit to the one side, and that despicable leader was bigger and stronger. Trumack dug in his boots, the shelf was covered in fine sand, and chunks of granite, and E-ri, in bare feet, could not get the needed foot hold.

Trumack twisted to face E-ri. Shock registered on his face, for just a second. He had not expected a third alien. Then, the two locked in a clenching dance, each trying to push the other over the edge.

****

Lee was fuming. It had taken them months to purchase the chickens, pigs, and their one cow, and here, these stupid soldiers were setting them all loose.

I have half a mind to let my dogs kill everyone of them...

But Poppa Loni had driven it home: 'Killing serves no purpose; the Maker will avenge us in time. We do not need to kill; merely defend.' And even as vicious as Lee's animals could be, they always held back, if Lee ordered it.

Lee wished he had a bigger pack. As soon as this was over, he resolved to increase; including the wild wolves.

In canine vision-speak, Lee sent the creatures he did have, chasing the men through the compound, and back out into the field. They fled for their lives, the dogs keeping so close, they couldn't even raise their guns to shoot, or to club.

With comforting sounds, and simple bird-talk, Lee gathered the frightened poultry, rabbits, and other livestock, shutting them safely again behind the barriers.

By the time he was finished, and set his dogs to guarding the perimeter, it was already near midnight. Lee headed inside.

****

Reuel was the heaviest, so he fell the fastest; his body turning, and shifting, as he fought to find some way to break his fall. The soldier's body caught the side of the diving, winged, black boy-bird, and Peek went spinning out of control.

Reuel also went careening, slamming hard against a nearby, granite wall, knocking the wind from the man. He continued in freefall, limp and unconscious.

Several minutes passed before Peek's equilibrium returned, so he could fly again. By then, the soldier had hit, with a splat, far below.

Peek's eyes now sought out his parents...

He was just in time to see Loni hit a ledge near the ground. The shelf broke his fall, but also, his back and neck.

Peek had no time to grieve.

Where is Momma Gem?

And then, he found her! Impaled by a broken upright, metal, beam, near the floor of the cavern.

Peek let out a screech that was near inhuman.

Chapter 33

Thea, with Nitha and Willow in tow, came visible in the large common room. It was empty, but...that wasn't all that had an absence to it.

Why are we disconnected? Why can I not feel the consciousness of my parents? And E-ri? He's confused...or panicked. He's never hysterical. Something is very wrong!

"Where is everyone?" wondered Willow.

Just then Storm entered from the kitchen, looking rattled and subdued.

"Where is everyone?" Willow challenged, again.

"Soldiers attacked while you were gone," Storm reluctantly offered, his voice sounding decidedly depressed. He turned away, as if ashamed.

"Did they win, or what?" Willow demanded. "Why do you act so...down?"

In a voice barely audible, he at last admitted: "I nearly killed...one of them..."

"Good!" exclaimed Nitha in mind-talk; a gut reaction, without thinking through to the consequences.

"Not good," he objected. "I'm as evil as they are..." His eyes dropped to his toes, and he refused farther comment.

Nitha knew he needed encouragement.

The girls looked at each other, as sudden empathy filled them. Hadn't they just come from their own failed attempt to mete out justice?

But, before anything more could be said, Lee pounced into the room, through the front door, disgust and just controlled anger in every move. Though he'd slunk in with the moves of a predatory cat, he was panting, as if he'd been either chased, or been pursing something.

"Stupid soldiers!" he exclaimed indignantly. "They set loose the whole barnyard; poultry flying everywhere...pigs, and rabbits all over the place. I just managed to get them all back in their corrals again."

His own problems forgotten, Storm quickly demanded: "Where are the soldiers now?"

"Ha!" laughed Lee. "Last time I saw them, they were hightailing across the fields with their tails between their legs."

"Yes!" Thea and Willow exclaimed together; Willow pumping her fist in the air. Then Thea broached the subject upmost in her mind.

"Where are Poppa Loni, and Momma? And what's wrong with E-ri?"

"Why?" chorused the others?"

"I can't sense them...only E-ri. And he, is petrified."

****

The scream-screech echoed through the cavernous space around them, turning Trumack's blood to ice. He pulled back from the blue-skinned boy he fought with, in livid shock.

To Trumack's mind, the sounds were those of many voices, a prelude of his impending doom. He imagined more bat-like men riding the tunnels toward him, capable of doing who knew what. The terrified soldier turned so swiftly, he near knocked E-ri over the edge. Then, Trumack headed pell-mell into the nearest side tunnel, running for his life, and not stopping until he was across the river, far, far away; lcaving E-ri kneeling on the edge of the precipice, his heart racing in dread.

E-ri had stopped, as if frozen in motion. For the first time in his life, the ice-skinned teen knew disconnect. Until this moment, he had always been connected to Loni or Gem, their minds a companionable background to everyday life, always there to instruct, comfort, or give advice. Never had he been alone...or lonely. He had parents...and Thea. But suddenly, it was like a vacuum had formed where their comfort had always been.

Because of their presence, he had never found real fear. He had been a reassured, confident, individual, always there to protect his siblings. Now, abruptly, he was cut adrift.

He knew, beyond a doubt...his fosters were dead. He was on his own...terror, dread, uncertainty, filled his soul.

But the ones he called Momma and Poppa had taught him well. One thing, he remembered, above all.

It was as if it was the last word instruction from the couple he so dearly loved:

'Take care of the others!'

****

Thea was in a panic. No matter how hard she probed, she could not connect with Gem or Loni. And E-ri's mind was cloudy...cloaked, keeping a disconnect, as if to protect her from something.

Thea shivered in dread. Something was very wrong.

They had found Brad desperately scanning the screens, showing the inside of the tunnels, but where ever Peek and E-ri were, they must have been out of camera range; so too, Gem and Loni. Also, there was no longer any sign of the two soldiers. No one had any inkling what had gone on. The tunnels were quiet...deathly so. All were imagining the worst.

"I'm going to go in," Thea finally decided.

"No!" Brad rounded on her. "Loni left me in charge. And I say, we don't want to lose anyone else. If they are alive, they will eventually come out..."

"But...I can't sense anyone, but E-ri..."

"All the more reason, for you to stay out of danger. He will come to us...when he can."

"What if he can't? What if he's hurt?"

"Doesn't matter. We don't know what's waiting in there. We wait!"

The children felt him inflexible; cold and unreasonable, yet...they obeyed.

All knew, what Brad suspected...

Epilogue:

It wasn't until days later, that Peek and E-ri emerged from the tunnel entrance under the waterfall. Lee had been searching along the river bed, in hopes of at least, a buried body, as had happened last time.

Even before the dogs let out the most unnerving, terrifying howl, Lee saw the pair emerge dragging two stretchers. The contents were covered over with tattered blankets, faces and all, so Lee knew the worst had happened.

His dogs were mourning like a pack of wild coyotes, and it wasn't just because, he had included the wild wolves among them. These animals had all known, and loved the ice-skinned couple. They were grieving a loss, irreplaceable.

As Lee ordered quiet, Thea sent the mind message to the other members, and everyone from inside abandoned their post, heading unerringly to that sandy shore.

By the time they had all arrived, the silence was eerily overwhelming.

It took only minutes, for E-ri to fill them in. His mind pictures were vivid; undiluted and stark. He was too angry to cushion his tale.

Tears did not come for some of them, until much later.

****

Brad and the seven teens, three female, and four male, stood beside the two new mounds of dirt in the graveyard. Tears streamed down gaunt faces, but hearts and minds boiled with anger, at the injustice perpetrated.

The cemetery had been prepared for Bella, as a memorial; the thought of expanding had not entered the young minds...least of all, to intern their beloved elders.

This is becoming an unacceptable occurrence!

When the soldier leader had fled, E-ri's one thought had been to get below to Loni, but it had taken more than a day to crawl down to the shelf, where Peek sat mourning. Both boys knew, it was useless to go to Gem; the girder had impaled her right through the heart.

Loni lay sprawled, at an unnatural angle; and Peek, though he'd flown to him immediately, seemed incapable of anything, but unrestrained grief.

E-ri knew the black boy blamed himself... Even he wondered, if he could have done something to arrive a little sooner.

When E-ri finally made it to the injured male, Loni was still breathing. E-ri's powers had returned slowly, but even the boy-teen knew, he did not have the power to heal this broken body, and getting Loni out into the open, to medical help, would be ineffective, too late, at best. The man did not regain consciousness. He breathed his last, in E-ri's arms, comforted by the presence of the sons he had fostered so diligently.

Hours after Loni had passed, E-ri finally realized, he was the one that needed to prod Peek.

Together, they rigged the stretchers, reverently took down the body of the only mother they had ever known; Peek flew with Loni's limp form to the floor of the cavern, and they both prepared the gruesome remains for the view of the rest of the family.

They did not even consider the body of the dead soldier; they ignored it; left it for the ravens, that flew in from outside, to pick clean the carcass. In their minds, it was fit recompense.

As the children turned away from the graves, and slowly meandered back to the compound above, Brad couldn't help wondering what the future held.

He shivered in dread.

What am I to do with them? How do I guide them? I am the only adult left. They are still so young...and different. They cannot be integrated into human society...not here on Earth. Here I am a human without powers, and I must guide...a menagerie of beings with talents beyond me. Oh, God! I am going to need your help.

His own two girls were the most normal...not really! Nitha was mute; Willow raised here. But both had displayed talents beyond mind-boggling. Then there were the others: Thea of the blue-skinned race; deadly. And E-ri, the same. And Lee with his beast-talent; Peek with wings, and last of all...Storm.

How will I be a beacon to these? Do I control, or let them find their own way?

###

About the Author:

If anything, Margaret Afseth is a survivor. She spent most of 2014 battling Cancer, a tumor pressing on the optic nerve. Now she counts herself among the rare few who, in her words, conquered the 'Beastie'. Though now of limited of vision, with the aid of her daughter to publish, she continues to write.

From an early age, she was making up stories. While raising her four children alone, she wrote her first novel...in long hand. Unfortunately, she gave the only copy of the manuscript to someone of the opinion, she should not be writing at all. He burned it.

Discouraged, she went underground, not surfacing again until her senior years, when at the age of seventy, 2013, she rewrote and published, as a three part series, the lost novel, calling it The Aopato Chronicles.

Since then, Margaret has gone on to write the Noor Chronicles, published 2014, the last book of which was written while she was undergoing Chemo and Radiation treatment.

This book is the last of the present Deception series. Who knows what may follow...

Discover other titles by Margaret Afseth at
Amazon.com
Aopato-book 1(Aopato Chronicles)
Remedy-book 2(Aopato Chronicles)
Turn Back-book 3(Aopato Chronicles)
Hidden From View(a short story)
Gentle Beast-book 1(Noor Chronicles)
Soul Saver-book 2(Noor Chronicles)
Healer Nest-book 3(Noor Chronicles)
Monsters Among Us-book 1(Deception Series)
Fire and Ice-book 2(Deception Series)

If you enjoyed this book, here is the Prologue of the first of a new series: watch for it.

WE ARE THE MONSTERS
By
Margaret Afseth

PROLOGUE:

Lee had always enjoyed life; that is until he, and his six foster brothers, and sisters had been thrown into the society of Earth. In this new world, the dominant creatures had no room for beings with their talents.

Lee talked to animals; he saw their beast visions and dreams; heard their simple mind-talk; could converse, and understand their aloud musing tongues. He had learned all this in the world where he'd been born; back on Azure Blue.

Then, there was his brother Peek, who could follow prey no matter how far it tried to run; he had wings, and could carry a sister or brother great distances.

And Storm; well his name spoke for itself...he could manipulate the weather.

And of course, there was E-ri, and sister Thea. Both could do most anything, the least of which was teleport.

They all had this way of talking in their heads; they had a sense of each other, even should they be far away.

But, this world feared such talents. Each being here lived separate; never connected.

****

The wild wolf pack milled at Lee's heels, restless to move forward. At present, they were stalking a young buck; it wasn't just for their satisfaction...the meat they brought down would be shared with the seven others in the communal settlement.

This bizarre family had just recently lost the pair who had raised them, to intruding soldier raiders, but though the young ones were still grieving, even though they were left all alone, life must carry on.

Now, there was but one adult left: Brad was originally from Earth; a human who, supposedly, would show them the ways of this new society...but, in their opinion, and from experience; it was debateable, whether this world was actually civilized...

****

Trumack had been having nightmares, and headaches; doing things he couldn't quite recall, or even why...he had done them. Sometimes...it was almost, as if, he were being controlled...

Ever since he had visited that Psychiatrist for his renewal referral; the one that had the appearance of an Egyptian, yet this other-worldly sense about him, the soldier had felt uneasy. The doctor had needlessly, and extensively, questioned him, when it was just a routine check-in; all about, not only his PTSD, but the whole story of his supposed encounter with aliens...on that other world. And...this man, unlike others, took his words as the gospel truth.

Almost, as if, he knew the place of which Trumack spoke, really existed.

****

The morgue was deadly still, and extremely cold, as the white coated attendant slid the gurney into the quiet, breath-freezing atmosphere of the room. The sheet-covered corpse gave no objection, as his bed was rammed accidentally against the doorframe.

Yet, a muted yell split the silence, as if he were, in fact, objecting.

The orderly's eyes went saucer size, but the sudden distant thumping, made him actually jump.

It sounded like kicking; the pounding coming from the furthermost drawer in the wall; screaming; muted, hoarse cries.

Gasping with fright, the man parked his stretcher born cargo against the wall, and hesitantly inched toward the sound. As he drew nearer, the kicking became more frantic. When he pulled out the freezer drawer, his shock was profound.

A livid physician confronted him; the man's fist just missing his face, as the doctor sat violently forward, and angrily sent a punch toward him.

He stepped back, aghast.

"Doctor Harmon?"

The large oncology physician had been missing almost a week; no one able to find him.

"What are you doing in here?"

Indignant, the physician simply cursed at him.

"Not your concern! Just let me out of here!"

TO CONTINUE READING GO TO AMAZON.COM

www.ingramcontent.com/pod-product-compliance
Lightning Source LLC
Chambersburg PA
CBHW021231020726
47498CB00008B/2799